Cory tapped on the window with his fingertips and hunched down. There was no response. He tried again, more loudly. In a moment, Carlotta was peering out at him.

"I'm leaving," he whispered. "I just wanted you to know."

Her dark eyes grew round. "Where?"

"I don't know," he answered, "but you can come with me if you want to."

Carlotta jerked back and grasped the window ledge with two thin hands. "I—I am an old woman," she faltered.

"You don't have to come. I mean, I'll understand if you don't. But I just thought you didn't belong here."

She stared. Staying there was making him nervous. Miss Sybil was sure to discover him. "Can you get out?" he asked.

"I can get out," Carlotta said slowly.

"An engaging tale that exposes, without wallowing in, the plight of the unwanted in our society."
—*Voice of Youth Advocates*

"This realistic, intergenerational narrative cuts through the issues of abandonment and the yearning for family to culminate in an upbeat resolution. . . . A good springboard for discussion."
—*Booklist*

THE GOLDEN DAYS

Gail Radley

Puffin Books

PUFFIN BOOKS
Published by the Penguin Group
Penguin Books USA Inc., 375 Hudson Street, New York, New York 10014, U.S.A.
Penguin Books Ltd, 27 Wrights Lane, London W8 5TZ, England
Penguin Books Australia Ltd, Ringwood, Victoria, Australia
Penguin Books Canada Ltd, 10 Alcorn Avenue, Toronto, Ontario, Canada M4V 3B2
Penguin Books (N.Z.) Ltd, 182–190 Wairau Road, Auckland 10, New Zealand

Penguin Books Ltd, Registered Offices: Harmondsworth, Middlesex, England

First published in the United States of America by
Macmillan Publishing Company, 1991
Published in Puffin Books, 1992

1   3   5   7   9   10   8   6   4   2

LIBRARY OF CONGRESS CATALOGING-IN-PUBLICATION DATA
Radley, Gail
The golden days / by Gail Radley.   p.   cm.
Summary: Convinced that his new foster parents do not really want
him, eleven-year-old Cory decides to run away with his new friend,
an elderly lady from the nearby nursing home.
ISBN 0-14-036002-6
[1. Foster home care—Fiction.   2. Old age—Fiction.
3. Friendship—Fiction.   4. Runaways—Fiction.]   I. Title.
[PZ7.R1223Go   1992]   [Fic]—dc20   92-19526

Printed in the United States of America
Set in Century Expanded

1

Cory squeezed into the backseat with Erica and Robert. In the front seat lounged Alonso. Their social worker, Ms. Hanks, was at the wheel.

"Hello, Cory. How are you?" When Ms. Hanks spoke, Cory imagined her words making musical bubbles that rose and rose and then, up out of sight, burst. "Michele's at the door waving good-bye. Michele's such a *nice* person. Did you wave, Cory?"

Cory gazed out the window at his new foster mother. She stood on the porch in her jeans and sweatshirt, one hand stuffed in her front pocket, the other waving hesitantly. She was too young to be a foster mother to an eleven-year-old, he thought. She was only thirteen when he was born.

He lifted his hand in a limp gesture and caught Ms. Hanks's eye in the rearview mirror. Ms. Hanks waved at Michele and eased the county car out onto the road.

"Well, you've been with Michele and Dan for a month now," said Ms. Hanks. "Are you enjoying it there?"

Cory glanced at the others. Alonso's dark head barely showed over the seat. Beside Cory, Robert drew his feet up onto the seat and wrapped his wiry arms around his knees. Erica, statuelike, fixed her eyes on the social worker's head and looked neither left nor right. Cory wondered what she saw in that tangle of hair.

Ms. Hanks peered back at them. "Robert, honey, don't put your feet on the upholstery. Do you like your new foster home, Cory?" she pressed.

"It's okay," Cory mumbled. He didn't like being asked about it in front of the other kids—but then, he didn't like talking about it away from them, either. Ms. Hanks would look into his face, searching for messages there, until Cory would have to turn his eyes away.

"The Keppermans are so glad to have you," Ms. Hanks continued. "You know, it's unusual for a couple their age to be foster parents. But they were so anxious. They took the training at the agency, and Michele has done volunteer work at the children's shelter."

I never saw her there, Cory thought. Probably she was there when he was at the Nortons' or the Sizemores'. How come it took training to be his foster parent, anyway? He knew he was a problem for Ms. Hanks—he was on his third foster home in only two years. He knew he was supposed to be grateful to have a home. And it was true that, when Cory arrived in August, Michele had switched to part-time work at the discount store to make more time for him. But why was she so awkward and quiet, then? It made him uncomfortable.

Dan was friendlier—more relaxed—but he worked a lot of overtime at the grocery, so Cory hadn't seen him as much.

It was okay at the Keppermans'. In fact, almost against his will, he sort of liked those two. But Cory felt it was inviting trouble to say so, especially to Ms. Hanks. It was better not to talk about feelings—or even feel them much. Cory imagined filing them away in a mental drawer labeled DANGEROUS MATERIAL.

Ms. Hanks swung into a parking space in front of Miss Sybil's Shady Rest. Cory sighed and opened the door. Robert scooted across the seat, seeming to catapult from the car. Alonso slunk out of the front seat, giving a noisy yawn. Erica stepped quickly out of her own door and attached herself to Ms. Hanks's elbow.

Cory was not looking forward to this. Last Saturday Ms. Hanks had made them rehearse two songs. Now they were supposed to sing them to the old people in this nursing home. It was one of Ms. Hanks's many screwy ideas. She called the group the Foster Friends Club. But they were not friends, only a handful of homeless kids who happened to be on Ms. Hanks's caseload. Ms. Hanks thought it would help them to spend their Saturdays doing good deeds. She was planning to write something about them for a social workers' magazine.

Ms. Hanks, with Erica on her arm, led them up the walk and into the building. It was a ranch-style house to which long, narrow sections had been added at different times.

Miss Sybil, who looked as if she'd been constructed from a stack of large, chunky toy blocks, squeaked toward them in white rubber-soled shoes. She ushered them into what she called the dayroom.

It looked to Cory like the living room of a house somebody was moving out of. There were two pictures on the wall, of the type Cory had seen stacked up in the discount store. One was of the Last Supper, the other of a craggy, snowcapped mountain. A couch and an easy chair faced the picture window, beneath which sat a large, old television. A piano rose against one bare wall. Against the opposite wall half a dozen wheelchair patients had been positioned.

Cory sucked in his breath. The air had a stuffy smell to it that made his stomach queasy.

Robert had attracted the attention of a wizened old woman who reached out a shaking, speckled hand to touch his hair. Robert whirled away, threw his arms around Cory's middle and tried to lift him up. "Get off!" Cory ordered, his face reddening. He shook himself free of Robert and moved away.

"Come on, kids," said Ms. Hanks. Herding them toward the picture window, she grouped them according to size and gave them song sheets. She settled herself at the piano and signaled them to begin.

"Come, come ye Saint,
no toil nor labor fear,"

Erica's and Robert's voices rang out in the room, Robert's high and squeaking like Miss Sybil's shoes. Alonso sang quietly and looked, without interest, out the window.

"But with joy, wend your way,
Though hard to you
this journey may appear,"

Cory raised and lowered his voice, trying to match it to Erica's and Robert's. To him, his voice sounded rusty and unused. Unlike Robert, who filled odd moments with random pieces of old and invented songs, Cory was not a singer. He glanced back at Ms. Hanks, who was watching them as she played. She lifted her chin twice—a gesture Cory knew meant "sing louder."

"Grace shall be as your day."

Cory looked away. The old people, whom Ms. Hanks had insisted would love this, gazed at them blankly. One man sat drooling onto his terry-cloth bathrobe. A woman drummed her fingertips on the tray attached to her wheelchair. Her drumming grew louder and louder but seemed to bear no relation to the music. Miss Sybil's was a creepy place.

> *" 'Tis better far for us to strive*
> *Our useless cares from us to drive;"*

Cory gave up singing and only mouthed the words. He hoped Ms. Hanks couldn't tell.

> *"Do this and joy*
> *Your hearts will swell!*
> *All is well! All is well!"*

He hated this song.

Miss Sybil led the applause. Stumping up in front of the group, she smacked her fleshy hands together and beamed at her residents. "Wasn't that lovely, Elsie? Did you hear that, Henry?"

"Thank you," said Ms. Hanks. "We have another song."

The next song on their sheet was "The Man on the Flying Trapeze." They had an inspirational song and a song to bring back good memories, Ms. Hanks had told them. Robert jerked up and down and swayed from side to side as they sang, as if he were the trapeze artist. The woman who had tried to pat him before pointed and said loudly, "Isn't that cute," at which Robert began bouncing and swaying harder still.

"Lovely, lovely," cried Miss Sybil as they finished. She turned to Ms. Hanks. "Is that all now?"

"Yes. We hope to learn more songs for next time."

"Wonderful. We have some refreshments, Ms. Hanks. Perhaps the children would like to serve them."

Ms. Hanks smiled. "I'm sure they would."

Cory was sure he wouldn't. Between the heaviness of the air and the old, glazed eyes watching him, he couldn't wait to get away. He felt leaden. He imagined himself running and running through a field of tall, swaying grass, even though he made it a point never to run anywhere unless absolutely necessary.

Ms. Hanks put a tray of drinks in his hands. Dixie cups filled partway with a bright green liquid. Lime Kool-Aid, he decided. He wondered if old people really liked Kool-Aid.

He offered drinks to the people on the couch, carefully avoiding their eyes as they accepted the drinks. Something about them frightened him. They were like rickety, storm-battered houses, their eyes like windows. He did not want to see inside.

The last person on the couch refused the drink he held out to her. "You do not like the trapeze song?" she asked.

7

Cory was startled into meeting the dark eyes that peered up at him. He hadn't expected anyone to speak to him. "It's okay," he mumbled.

"You did not sing it," the woman pointed out.

"I don't like to sing."

She nodded and took an oatmeal cookie from the tray Robert held out to her. "I do not sing here, either," she said.

Cory was relieved when Ms. Hanks finally drove them home. The Keppermans' house was only a few blocks from the nursing home, so Cory was the first one dropped off.

Slamming the door on Ms. Hanks's farewell, he bounded up the walk to the rambling old frame house, still trying to shake off the pall of the nursing home. He was looking forward to turning the radio in his room up loud and driving the words of Ms. Hanks's stupid songs out of his mind.

"Cory? That you?" Michele came out of the kitchen, wiping her hands on a dish towel. "How 'bout some cookies? I just made a batch of oatmeal raisin."

"I had some at the nursing home."

"Oh." Michele wound the towel around her hand. "Well, how was it?"

"Dumb. I don't know why I have to do it." He looked up at her from beneath a fringe of long blond bangs. He imagined she could not look into his eyes that way.

"Well, I guess you don't *have* to. You could tell Ms. Hanks you'd rather not."

Cory shrugged. He did have to do it, he thought. If he didn't, Ms. Hanks would get upset. She would ask him what was bothering him. There would be talk and more talk. Maybe she'd even bring it up in front of the other kids. Maybe she'd decide he ought to move to *another* foster home. The thought of more bouncing around wearied him. "It doesn't really matter," he said.

"They used to take us to a nursing home to sing at Christmas. The people really seemed to enjoy it."

"Who took you?"

"The Girls' Home."

"The Girls' Home?" Cory squinted at her. "What girls' home?"

"In Randall. That's where I grew up." Michele's eyes slid away. "Are you sure you don't want some cookies?"

Cory shook his head. He wondered if she was making the story up. You could never be sure when an adult was making something up to get on a kid's good side.

The kitchen timer rang.

"That's the second batch ready," said Michele, starting for the kitchen. She seemed suddenly as anxious to get away as Cory felt. "You can lick the bowl, if you like."

"Nah. I got stuff to do."

In his room, Cory flopped down on the bed. He turned the radio up all the way, even though that had been a complaint of Mrs. Norton, his last foster mother, even though Ms. Hanks had lectured him about being considerate after he'd had to leave the Norton home.

He liked the way the beat pulsated through the room, pounding through his body. He liked the way it drove thoughts from him. He wondered briefly if Michele would come and tell him to turn it down.

She did not.

2

On Sunday Cory and Dan had planned to go down to the school yard and toss a football around. It was Cory's experience that foster fathers, within the first month of his arrival, extended an invitation to "go off like a couple of guys" together.

With Mr. Norton he had sat through a high-school football game, consuming more hot dogs, candy, and Coke than he wanted. Mr. Norton shivered in the night air, pulling his hat low and turning his collar up. Cory suggested that they go back to the house, but Mr. Norton cried out in mock horror that they couldn't leave in the middle of the game. He wrapped his coat more tightly around himself and asked Cory to explain parts of the game he said he had forgotten.

Before that, it had been Mr. Sizemore and a fishing trip. They sat for hours in a rickety boat, not talking and scarcely moving for fear of scaring the fish away. Cory went home with a string of sad-looking little stripers and a vow never to go off alone with Mr. Sizemore again.

His own father he could barely remember—just the black zippered sleeve of his leather jacket, the crunch of gravel beneath his boots, and the way he stomped on his motorcycle to get it going. And then there was the vision of the accident that killed him when Cory was five. Cory wasn't sure whether he actually had seen it happen or if it was a nightmare that kept repeating itself. The black-gloved hands and helmeted face loomed closer and closer until the whole picture shattered like chips in a kaleidoscope. He did not remember any outings with his father.

Dan did not talk about "us guys" going off. In fact, he invited Michele, who smiled and said, "Maybe next time."

Cory was waiting in the car for Dan to return with the cooler that held their sandwiches and drinks when he heard the telephone ring. Moments later, Dan appeared without the cooler.

"Hey, buddy, guess what?" Dan said.

"What?"

"The grocery called. One of the guys called in sick at the last minute. I gotta work."

Cory got out of the car. Dan probably didn't even want to go, he thought. This little outing was just something he had concocted for "getting closer to the boy." Dan was just like Mr. Norton, shivering through the football game, wondering what it was all about, and Mr. Sizemore, who would have been happier fishing alone. He was probably glad to get out of it.

"I told 'em, 'Hey, can't I at least have Sunday off?' But they're heartless. Umm, I won't be back till around ten tonight. But maybe Tuesday, after school—"

"It doesn't matter." Cory cut him off.

"Cory, I'm sorry—"

"Forget it." Cory looked away and headed for the house.

"Hey, Cory—"

Cory walked past Michele, who looked quickly at him and went out to Dan.

Over the radio Cory could barely hear the sound of the car pulling away. In a moment, Michele appeared in his doorway. Cory, propped up against the two fluffy pillows on his bed, looked at her and then turned the radio down.

"Dan was really sorry he had to cancel on you, Cory," she said.

Cory lowered his eyelids and shrugged. "I don't care about throwing around a stupid football."

"You know, I'm not bad at it myself. Dan and I play catch together a lot."

Cory didn't answer.

"We could go—you and I." She hesitated and then came in to sit on the edge of his bed. "Dan really

---

13

wanted to spend time with you. But we just need the money so bad. That's why he's been gone so much."

Cory stood up. "I said don't worry about it." The more she talked about it, the more he felt tears burning around the edges of his eyes, and that made him madder still. He started toward the door. Michele twisted around to look at him but did not get up. "I'm going for a walk."

He was disgusted with himself for the emotions that had threatened to spill over, and for being disappointed in the first place. What made it worse was that Dan and Michele had seen it. He walked quickly away from the house, holding his head high in case Michele was watching from the window.

He didn't care about the Keppermans and their stupid football. It was dumb to get attached to people who were just going to dump you when you got in the way, like Mrs. Norton, or desert you like—like his mother.

Thinking of her was something he had vowed not to do. He kicked at a stone. Unfortunately, he could remember her much better than he could remember his father. She had been with him longer—until he was nine. He remembered her staring out the window for what seemed like hours, while he tugged at her hand and begged her to play. He remembered burying his face in her long blond hair while she rocked him, and how her face twisted up when she screamed at him. He remembered chasing her down the stairs and running after that beat-up old Volkswagen van until he could run no more. He remembered the hollow feeling when he realized she wasn't going to stop and he couldn't catch up to her—and how he wished for tears to fill up that well of fear and pain. But the tears did not come until nightfall. She had put a loaf of bread, a jar of peanut butter, and a jar of Marshmallow Fluff on the kitchen table and walked out of his life.

Cory saw a patch of woods and headed for it. It occurred to him that Michele might look for him. She'd try to get him talking, like Ms. Hanks did. But she probably wouldn't go into the woods.

The woods was a good place to be—all cool shadows and strips of light. That was one good thing about staying at the Keppermans'—this little hideaway was nearby.

He walked, kicking stones, until the anger and disappointment had eased. When he went back to the house, his face would be blank. If they thought he cared before, they would decide they were wrong. Caring meant hurting, and he wasn't about to get hurt by Dan and Michele Kepperman.

Just as he was about to kick one last rounded rock, he saw legs, a head, and a tiny tail slide out. He bent over the turtle. He picked it up and instantly the legs and tail withdrew, and the head disappeared behind a trapdoor.

Cory set the turtle down and watched it. He hadn't had a pet since the blue-tailed skink at the Nortons'. Blue had gotten away from him in the basement, and ever after Mrs. Norton had turned on all the lights and stomped loudly down the basement steps for fear she might surprise the lizard out of his hiding place. Cory was never able to find him.

The turtle slowly opened its shell a crack, peered out with sharp little orange eyes, and closed it again. This was one pet that wouldn't run away.

Cory picked the turtle up and headed for a clearing. There was a house ahead. He figured he could cut through the yard, and then he'd be just a couple of blocks from the Keppermans'. He was anxious to make a home for Mr. T and feed him. Mr. T—that was a good name for a turtle. A strong name.

He was halfway across the yard when he noticed an old woman on the patio watching him. "Okay if I cross the lawn?" he called.

"Suit yourself."

"Thanks." Maybe tomorrow he could find Mr. T a mate. Then he'd have a family of baby T's.

"What is that you have?" the old woman asked.

"A turtle. I found it in the woods."

"Bring it here."

Cory hesitated.

"Come. I will not bite."

As Cory approached the old woman, he realized he was cutting across the rear of Miss Sybil's Shady Rest. The old woman was the one who had spoken to him on Saturday. She was a small, thin woman; with her long skirt rippling in the breeze, she reminded Cory of a scarecrow. Her thick gray-and-white hair was gathered in a band and flowed down her back.

"You are the boy who came not to sing yesterday," she remarked.

Cory smiled a bit in spite of himself. "Yeah."

She eyed the turtle critically. "What does it do?" she sniffed. "Nothing but hide."

Cory put the turtle down in the grass. "He can walk around and eat," he said defensively.

"Does not seem like much of a pet. I had a lion once. She could swallow that turtle without blinking."

"Oh right, a lion." This old lady was weird, Cory decided. Or maybe she was trying to make fun of him.

The woman sat down on a rusty glider. The seat barely quivered under her slight weight. "It was not mine, really," she admitted. "It was the lion tamer's. But this lion—Zeba—she knew me. She looked for me. She was a great, fierce creature."

"What lion tamer?"

She looked at him with impatience. "In the circus."

"You weren't with the circus!"

"I was."

"Aw, c'mon!" Cory was mistrustful. How could someone who was with the circus end up as a scrawny old lady in a nursing home?

"Well, who do you think runs the circus? Robots?" she demanded, her black eyes snapping. "Those little beepy things on the games you kids play?"

"I guess somebody has to run the circus," he

conceded. He still wasn't sure that he should believe her. "What did you do in the circus?"

"Different things. I started out selling cotton candy when I was sixteen. Then I was the magician's assistant. Then I was the fortune-teller." She sighed, looking across the manicured lawn. "After that, the circus changed. I did many things—cook, costumes, many things."

"Fortune-teller," Cory repeated. "You want to read my palm? Or look into a crystal ball?" He was half teasing and half wondering what she might tell him.

"What is your name, boy?"

"Cory Wainwright."

"Well, Cory Wainwright, I do not do much of that anymore. I am just an old lady. An old lady in the house of death."

Cory saw an elderly man shakily making his way through the sliding glass doors onto the patio. With every step he placed a metal walker before him. Old people made him feel sad and sick and scared all at the same time. And this old lady was creepy.

"Look, Cory Wainwright, your turtle is running away."

Cory looked where she pointed her crooked forefinger. The turtle had come out of its shell and was lumbering across the patio as quickly as it could.

"It wants to be free," said the old woman. "It does not want to be your pet."

"He does, too," Cory objected. "He's just getting

his exercise." He grabbed the turtle. Head and legs disappeared within the shell. Only a little gray tail protruded. Cory touched it and it curled inside.

"It wants to be free," she repeated. "Everything wants to be free—you, me, that old turtle, Zeba."

"So I suppose you let your lion go."

The woman pressed her lips together. "I thought of it."

"I've got to be leaving," Cory said abruptly. He wasn't so sure he liked this old lady. He started across the lawn again.

"Good-bye, Cory Wainwright."

Cory glanced back at her but did not reply.

3

Cory had to admit that Michele took to turtles a lot better than Mrs. Norton took to lizards. Mrs. Norton didn't even like to look at Blue. Michele, on the other hand, sat on the floor of Cory's room reading from an old encyclopedia while Mr. T tentatively explored.

"Did you know sea turtles can swim twenty miles an hour?" she asked, bending over the volume. "And the smooth soft-shelled turtle can outrun a man on level ground."

Cory considered Mr. T, who was raised up on his stumpy forefeet, peering over Cory's sneaker. "He doesn't look very athletic to me."

Michele laughed, and Mr. T jerked inward. "Yes, well, he's a box turtle. Maybe he's more a philosopher."

"What does he eat?"

20

Michele read further. "Almost anything, it says, but they especially like fruits. And I know they eat garden vegetables."

She helped Cory make a mound of apple shavings, which they placed in a long, low box, along with Mr. T.

Mrs. Norton had insisted that Blue be kept outside—a rule Cory had broken to play with him in the basement. But Michele had no objection when Cory wanted to keep Mr. T's box by the end of his bed.

There Cory could lie on his bed and watch his pet. There wasn't a lot to watch. Mr. T stayed rooted to one spot most of the time, peering cautiously out of his peephole with grave, unblinking eyes.

Maybe he was just feeling fat and satisfied in his new home. Cory made a path of raisins across the bottom of his box. Like Hansel and Gretel, Mr. T could eat as he walked, each step making him more content. He should be agreeable about walking for his food. Even turtles needed exercise, didn't they?

But Mr. T didn't seem particularly interested in eating, either. Cory decided he was lonely, so after school a few days later he went to the woods to find a Mrs. T. He spent an hour walking quietly and watchfully but saw no turtles. It was a misty, gray day. The dampness crept through his jacket, chilling him. Perhaps turtles hid themselves under leaves or in holes when the weather was bad, Cory thought.

He was picking his way out of the woods when he saw the old woman from the nursing home coming toward him. He stopped to watch her moving slowly through the mist, wondering if she had seen him. What was she doing out there, anyway? He turned to go back through the woods.

"Is that Cory Wainwright?"

"It's me." He paused. What did she want with him?

"What are you poking around here about? Did you bring that turtle back?"

"He's at the house." Cory waited, but she didn't reply. "He's lonely, so I'm looking for another."

The woman nodded. "Peter-John thought that would be enough. But I wasn't ready to be trapped then."

"Who's Peter-John?"

"Well, Peter-John, the roustabout. Married the ticket girl instead."

Cory felt confused. "What's a roustabout?"

"He puts up the tents and takes them down. I was not ready to move to New Jersey, to wash the dishes and mind the babies."

"Car-lot-ta!" Miss Sybil's voice cut through the damp air.

Cory and the woman looked toward the nursing home. Miss Sybil was trundling toward them, wrapping a sweater around her broad, fleshy shoulders.

"You come tomorrow," the old woman whispered urgently. "I will show you my scrapbook from the circus. You come to the patio again in the afternoon."

"Is that your name—Carlotta?" Cory wanted to know.

"Yes."

Cory didn't much like calling grown-ups by their first names. They usually only invited you to do that when they were trying to get you to trust them. Like Ms. Hanks. "Call me Patsy," she said in that super-cheery way of hers. And as soon as he began to trust her a little, she was jerking him around like a dog on a chain. It hadn't taken him long to go back to calling her Ms. Hanks. If Dan and Michele didn't look so much like overgrown kids, he'd told himself, he'd be calling them Mr. and Mrs., too.

"What's your last name?" he asked the old woman.

She passed a bony hand across her wrinkled brown face. "Just Carlotta," she said.

Miss Sybil caught up to them then. "Why, Carlotta, dear," she chirped. "What on earth? You're going to catch your death—" She looked quickly at Cory. "Aren't you one of the boys who came to sing—one of Ms. Hanks's children?"

Cory noted that there was a change in her tone when she spoke to him. Suspicious, he thought. Disapproving. "Yes," he replied, careful to stand straight and look steadily at her. He didn't want her to think he was frightened.

"You ought to go on home now. This is a quiet place. A place for the elderly. You come back when

Ms. Hanks brings you to sing." She gave him a brief, narrow smile and put a protective arm around Carlotta, guiding her gently, but firmly, toward the building. "Now Carlotta, you mustn't wander off like that. And to these woods! My land, there could be snakes about, and nasty little beetles and bugs!"

Carlotta looked over her shoulder as she was being led away. "Still not ready, Cory Wainwright. Still not," she said.

He wasn't about to let Miss Sybil tell him what to do. She wasn't his boss. Carlotta had invited him to visit and he guessed she had a right to see whomever she wanted. She wasn't a prisoner, after all. And he couldn't help but be curious about this strange old woman who claimed to have been with the circus.

He found Carlotta pacing the patio. When she saw him, her face broke into a wrinkled smile.

"So, you're here. Come, my young friend Cory." She sat down on the glider and patted the spot beside her. Cory sat down. She picked up the box at her feet, set it on her lap, and lifted the lid. Within was a small scrapbook, loose newspaper clippings, posters, a plume, and bits of cloth and bright jewelry.

Cory picked up a poster. "The Philo Demetrius Circus," he read. "Was that the circus you belonged to?"

"It was. It was like the circuses of the early days—a real circus. Now this picture"—she held up a newspaper photo,—"this was Anatole, the trapeze artist. How the crowds gasped at his somersaults and pirouettes! And his wife, Gabriella, she was wonderful." Tenderly she picked up the pink plume and stroked it. "They worked together, and one night—I remember it like today—she was doing her pirouettes. Her timing was wrong. Oh, Anatole told her not to perform that night—she had flu. But Gabriella would not stay away. She fell and broke her neck. At her funeral Anatole gave each of us one of her plumes."

"Why didn't she have a net?"

"There was a net. But, Cory, nets are not soft. You must know how to land. Gabriella knew, of course, but not that night."

Cory looked up and saw Miss Sybil gazing at them from behind the glass door. Carlotta looked up. She frowned. "Do not mind her." She opened the scrapbook.

"Aren't you supposed to have visitors?"

"Of course. She is a prune."

Miss Sybil slid the door open and came toward them. "Young man, can I help you?"

"I am helping him," Carlotta cut in. "We are visiting. Now let me be, Sybil. It is not cold and you should find another chick to cluck over."

Miss Sybil straightened. "It will soon be medicine time, Carlotta," she said stiffly.

"Those pills will keep. I will be along."

Miss Sybil sucked in her breath, glaring at her. Then she turned on her heel and left.

"She sure butts in," Cory remarked.

"She has no life but to fuss and make us miserable." Carlotta turned a page in the book, but she seemed to have lost interest in it. She looked across the lawn.

Cory picked up a photo that had not been glued down. A handsome young man in work clothes smiled into the camera. "Who's this?"

"Hmm?" Carlotta shifted her gaze. "That is Peter-John." She passed her hand across her eyes. "None of us have lives here."

Cory tried to imagine Carlotta being as young as the man in the picture, to erase the lines that crisscrossed her face, to fill in the hollows of her cheeks, to straighten her narrow back. She was probably kind of pretty, he decided, though not in a Hollywood sort of way. He turned the photo over. There was writing on the back, but before he could read it, she had taken the picture from him and put the lid on the box.

"Tell me about you now," she said.

"Me? There's nothing much about me."

"Of course there is. You live near here? You go to school?"

"I'm in a foster home near here." She looked blankly at him, so he explained. "My father died when I was little and my mother dumped me, so now I have to live with other people. Foster parents." He had practiced telling his story. Now it rolled off his tongue easily, without pain.

"They are good people?"

Cory felt a sudden sense of unease. They did seem to be good people, he grudgingly admitted to himself. Dan had kept his promise about tossing the football with him. They'd stayed at the school yard Tuesday evening until almost dark. They'd even played a little tackle. Once, when Dan lunged at him, Cory glimpsed a classmate passing by and felt a surge of triumph. Cory was an outsider at school. But this boy was seeing him looking as if he belonged. Cory tackled Dan and they tumbled halfway down the hillside, locked together. Afterward, they fell back on the grass, laughing and gasping for breath.

And Michele, despite her silences and obvious discomfort, did have bursts of enthusiasm, like with the turtle. She tried to do things for him, too, like baking, or making his bed when it was supposed to be his job.

But these were private feelings, the kind that seemed to grow bigger when you talked about them, and made you hurt more when things went wrong. "The Keppermans are okay," he told Carlotta. "I don't feel like talking about them."

"Well, what about school?"

"I'm in the fourth grade. I'm eleven years old and in the fourth grade." This was something that disgusted him. He didn't look like a fourth-grader. He looked like the sixth-grader he should have been, and he always felt like a big jerk in class.

Carlotta made no comment. Maybe she didn't even know eleven-year-olds had no business in fourth grade.

"I'm not dumb," he added. "I just flunked a couple of times from moving around so much." It was only partly true. He wasn't dumb, and he had moved around. But even he recognized that that was not entirely responsible for his failures.

"You do not sing, you do not do schoolwork. What is it that you do, Cory Wainwright, besides imprison small, frightened creatures?"

Cory scowled. She was making fun of him. One minute she was nice and the next she was crabby. "Yeah, well, at least I'm not a prisoner in this dump," Cory snapped, "with Miss Sybil tagging after me like a baby-sitter!"

Cory cast one angry glance back at her and trotted off toward the woods, yanking a fistful of leaves from a low-hanging branch as he went.

Something had happened at the Keppermans'. The air seemed charged with untold news, and Michele was as near to being bubbly as Cory could imagine. When Cory flopped on the couch to watch television after dinner, Michele headed for her room, and Cory saw her beckon Dan to follow. They closed the door.

Cory sat up. The Nortons were always disappearing like that—especially just before they called Ms. Hanks to take him back to the children's shelter.

There had been excited talking and crying behind the closed doors, and when Mrs. Norton came out she was red eyed and would not look at him. Cory could never figure out which one of them wanted to get rid of him, but he supposed both of them would have been happier with a pigtailed three year old. He wondered why they'd agreed to take him in the first place.

Cory rose and padded to his bedroom in his stocking feet. He left the TV on so Michele and Dan would think he was still watching. He gently eased himself down onto the bed, which was against the wall shared by the two rooms. It was hard to make out their words. Cory sucked in his breath.

". . . a baby," he heard Michele say. ". . . the doctor . . ."

"Oh, honey, that's great!" said Dan. ". . . thought we couldn't . . ."

"I know . . . real family of our own . . ."

There was silence, and then, ". . . about Cory . . ." Dan had dropped his voice. Cory pressed his ear against the wall.

". . . not yet . . ." he heard Michele say.

Now they seemed to have moved to a different part of the room, and Cory could not catch what they were saying. He sat on the edge of the bed and looked into Mr. T's box. Mr. T was wedged into one corner, his unblinking orange eyes staring at the cardboard walls. He'd been like that for two days.

He wondered suddenly if Mr. T was a girl. Maybe he was a girl and about to have babies. "When you're pregnant," he'd once heard someone say, "nothing else matters."

He didn't matter, either, Cory thought darkly. They weren't going to spring it on him right away. They'd wait till he got more used to being there, till he'd begun thinking of the Keppermans' as home. Then they'd tell him, "Sorry, kid. We're going to have a *real* family now. You were just a pretend kid to us. So pack your bags, kiddo. It's back to the shelter with you."

Cory went to the closet and lifted his backpack off the hook. Well, he wasn't going to let them call all the shots. He opened his dresser drawers and began to stuff clothes into the pack.

There wasn't much to packing, Cory thought. Not for a foster kid. You never had time to collect a bunch of junk like other kids. You never got in trouble for having a messy room, because you didn't own enough stuff to make a mess. You traveled light; maybe that was best.

No, Cory thought, setting his filled pack on the closet floor, he wouldn't let them ruffle him. When they gave him the word, he'd just pick up that back-pack and hoist it over his shoulder. "Hey," he'd say, all cool and casual, "it's nothing to me. I been waitin' for weeks to get out of this place."

4

"Cory! Cory Wainwright!"

Cory jerked his head up. He had been kicking the same rock along the sidewalk for nearly a block. He had focused all his attention on kicking it, first with one foot and then the other. Now his concentration was broken. He saw Carlotta scuffing across the nursing home lawn toward him, her long raspberry-and-black skirt swirling about her legs.

"Will you go to the store for me?" she asked urgently. She held out a scrap of paper and a crinkled five-dollar bill.

Cory looked at her and frowned. This crazy old lady could not seem to remember that he was mad at her. That she'd insulted him and he'd yelled at her and stomped off. He glanced at the paper. " 'Two cups unhulled sesame seeds and coriander'?" he read.

"Roasted, if you can find them. Or I will have to get into the kitchen at night. I will probably be caught."

"Roasted what—sesame seeds?"

"Of course. Coriander is a spice."

"You mean sesame seeds like on hamburger buns?"

Carlotta took a furtive look behind her. "Yes. You will do it? I have everything else I need hidden in my room."

"What are you making?" Cory couldn't imagine what anybody could do with two cups of sesame seeds. They had no taste.

"Halvah," she said impatiently. "I am making halvah."

"What the heck is halvah?"

"It is Turkish candy." She turned to look behind her again and saw Miss Sybil heading toward them. "I will give you some. Will you go?"

"Yeah, I guess. Is that where you're from? Turkey?"

"No."

Miss Sybil had lumbered up beside them now and was frowning at the note and money in Cory's hand.

"Carlotta, you're not out here giving away your money, are you?"

"No, I am here talking to a young friend," Carlotta said curtly. "Is that all right with you?"

"But I saw you hand money to him. I wasn't aware you were keeping money in your room, dear.

Young man"—her voice grew stern as she turned to Cory—"I don't know what she's told you, but it's not right to take advantage of the elderly. They often don't do what's best for themselves."

She reached out to take the money from him. Cory drew back, his fingers clenching the bill.

"I don't know what you're talking about, lady," he lied. "This is my money."

Carlotta shot a grateful look at him and turned back to Miss Sybil, her black eyes snapping.

"Now young man, I've asked you not to come around here. I can't imagine what you're after. I don't want to have to call Ms. Hanks and ask her to move you from this neighborhood. Give me the money and be on your way."

Cory bristled. He looked quickly into Miss Sybil's steel-gray eyes. He knew her type. She was the kind who boxed you into corners, all the while smiling and telling you how good it would be for you. He jammed the money into his pocket and ran. "I'll do it, Carlotta," he yelled back over his shoulder.

He could hear Carlotta cursing Miss Sybil as he rounded the corner.

"Cory!" Michele was calling from the kitchen. "You think Mr. T would like a cabbage leaf?"

Cory leaned against the doorway. "I don't know. He doesn't seem to be eating much."

"Think he's depressed? Maybe he wants to go home."

Cory winced. What could Mr. T possibly have against him to make him want to run away? "I was wondering if maybe he's a girl and going to have babies."

Michele looked up quickly, and Cory blushed. He thought he detected a smile playing on her lips.

"I'll try the cabbage," Cory decided. "If he has babies soon, then we'll know what was wrong."

Cory laid the curved green cabbage leaf on top of Mr. T, making a little cave of it. He could eat his way out.

On Cory's dresser sat a narrow jar of coriander and a little brown bag of roasted sesame seeds. For the seeds, he had had to go to the health food store, searching its shelves of whole wheat spaghetti, Tiger's Milk, and natural vitamins.

He slipped on his jacket, put the seeds and spice in his pocket, and started toward the front door. "I'll be back in a few minutes," he said.

"Dinner in half an hour, Cory," said Michele.

"Okay."

He approached the nursing home through the woods so that Miss Sybil would not see him. The sun had edged down below the horizon, and the shadows in the woods were deepening. Now, at the woods' edge, came the gray expanse of lawn and then the nursing home, its windows like so many glowing eyes.

Cory, crouching, hesitated. He had not thought of how to find her. She had always been outside, finding him. Where in the building her room was he had no idea.

In a sudden burst of faith, he darted out of the sheltering woods, crossed the lawn, and hunched up in the shadow of the building's rear wing. The thick, warm smell of stew reached out to him, and he heard the clattering and rolling of a food cart.

He inched upwards and peered through the window. An old man, a caved-in and hollow creature, picked at the food on his tray. Cory hunched down and scooted along with bent knees.

In the next room a woman dressed in white had stopped the food cart to deliver dinner to a gray-haired woman. Cory ducked and moved on.

Two more windows and no Carlotta. But in the last window, the one nearest the main part of the building, there was a rectangle of darkness within the light. Cory made his way to it and, leaning back, read the poster propped in the window: PHILO DEMETRIUS CIRCUS! Cory raised his head. "Pssst!" he hissed. "Carlotta!" He felt his heart beat faster as he recalled Miss Sybil's threat to complain about him to Ms. Hanks. She would surely do it if she found him lurking in the shrubbery, calling to Carlotta. He peeked in and hissed again.

Carlotta heard him this time and came to the window.

"Raise the screen," Cory whispered. "I've got your stuff."

Pressed against the building, he heard muttering and the sounds of a struggle above. Then there came another voice.

"Carlotta, what are you doing, dear?" The voice rose and fell in notes of false concern and veiled displeasure. The voice was Miss Sybil's.

Cory drew in his breath.

"I want some fresh air," said Carlotta loudly.

"You've plenty of air, dear. And we wouldn't want to open the screen to bugs now, would we? Why don't you lie down, dear, and rest awhile."

Cory waited. The yard grew darker. Here and there lights blinked out. The sounds of televisions playing on several different stations flowed out into the night air. Cory's folded legs grew stiff. He touched the bag of sesame seeds in his pocket. Then he saw a dark figure on the patio. It was a slight figure. The length of the skirt gave her away.

Cory made his way quickly to Carlotta and handed her the packages. She tucked them within the folds of her skirt. Her hair was splayed out on her back and shoulders. In the moonlight her face was luminous. Her look held him like an embrace.

"You come tomorrow at four," she said. "In the woods. I will give you halvah then."

"Tomorrow at four," he repeated.

He closed the door of the Kepperman home. His nostrils were besieged by the warm mingled aromas of cabbage and beef. On the table sat dishes and glasses in pristine cleanness.

Michele burst out of the kitchen. "Where have you been?"

Cory's shoulders jerked upward, as if preparing for defense. "For a walk."

"You said you'd be a few minutes. It's been an hour and a half." Michele wrung her hands—a gesture Cory had only seen done by cartoon characters.

"I guess I lost track of time."

Michele let out her breath in uneven little gusts. For a moment she seemed to waver, and Cory thought she would run and embrace him. He folded one arm across his chest, grasping the other arm.

"We were worried," said Michele. "We waited dinner for you."

"You could've gone ahead without me."

"We want to have dinner together like a family," Michele explained. "And now Dan's gone out looking for you."

Just then the door swung open and Dan strode in. "Did he—" He saw Cory and stopped. His eyebrows drew together.

"He just got here," Michele told him.

"Cory, what's the big idea—"

"I've already talked to him about it, Dan. Let's just eat. I've probably heated all of the juice out of the beef by now."

Cory suddenly had no appetite for dinner, and

neither, it seemed, did Michele or Dan, despite their long wait. Michele lapsed into a troubled silence, picking at her food. Dan, after vigorously sawing at his corned beef, laid down his fork and knife as if to speak. Then, with a glance at Michele, he stopped himself and thoughtfully resumed his dinner.

I'm a lot of trouble to them, Cory thought. I bet they wish I hadn't come.

5

The halvah was grainy and pale. Cory bit and it crumbled in his mouth—a sweet, mysterious flavor. "It's great!" he announced.

Carlotta, seated on the trunk of a fallen tree, smiled and offered him more from the plastic bag on her lap.

Cory took another square and asked, "Did Miss Sybil see you go into the woods?"

Carlotta shook her head. "She is showing some poor old soul's children around the place. Everything circles around, it seems. The children become the parents and lock their parents in their rooms."

"Are you guys supposed to be prisoners? What would Miss Sybil do to you for coming out here?"

"One man calls too often for the bedpan. They give him an extra sleeping pill now. It is true. I heard the nurses say so." She looked at him, unblinking.

On the patio, Cory could see a woman bent practically in half as she inched her way to the glider. He moved over a bit so the tree would block him.

"What I don't get is why you're at Miss Sybil's," said Cory. "You don't seem like you belong there."

"I do not belong anywhere, but what has that to do with where I am?"

Understanding rumbled. Cory knew what it was not to belong anywhere. Somebody sticks you someplace and tells you, "This is where you belong," but you don't, really. It's just where you are.

Carlotta straightened her back as if shaking a weight off her shoulders. "Give me your hand," she said. "Today, I will read your palm."

"I thought you were done with that."

"I will do it because you are my friend."

She took his outstretched hand in hers and squinted into its etched palm. "I see many branched lines," she said, after a moment. "This means that you are sensitive and troubled. The heart line is short and marked like a chain." She looked up. "You have a suspicious nature, and because of this, troubles in love."

Cory squinted down at his palm, trying to see what Carlotta saw there.

"This branch is your life line," she went on. "It shows travel. Your head line is deep and long. You think deeply about many things." She released his hand.

"What else?" Cory prompted.

40

"It is enough. It tires me, this concentrating. And I forget things. In many ways, though, Cory," she added, "your palm is like mine."

With a shiver, Cory stuffed his hands into his pockets. "How did you get into this nursing home?"

Carlotta's eyes closed, and she hugged herself. "I had a heart attack. The doctor at the hospital sent me here. He said I was getting too old and forgetful to live alone."

"Didn't you have anything to say about it?"

Carlotta opened her eyes. "The old and sick have nothing to say," she answered flatly.

"But you're okay now, aren't you?" he persisted. "You could go home now."

"I have no home. This is the house of death. You don't go home from here." Beneath the surface of her words, a current of anger flowed. Cory knew that anger.

Grasping, Cory said, "What about your family? Couldn't you go with them?"

"I have no family. The doctor said I would be glad to have people around. He said they would be good for me."

"Are they?"

"I have not met any yet who are. Everyone here is waiting to die. Impatiently waiting."

In Cory's heart an unexpected spirit of generosity surged. "I'll be your family," he said.

Carlotta looked at him solemnly. "And I will be yours."

Something akin to joy filled Cory up and threatened to spill over. Carlotta filled his pockets with halvah and picked her way across the barren yard. Cory raced toward the Keppermans'. In the headiness of this strange emotion, he took an experimental jump for joy. It felt good.

At the door, he reassembled his feelings and waited for the pounding of his heart to cease.

The Keppermans had more dreary thoughts on their minds.

"The school called today, Cory. Said you've been having trouble." Dan's face was grave.

Michele, sitting with her knees locked to her chest, looked out the window.

Cory lurched into a different, plodding time zone. The transition made him feel a little dizzy. He saw his school desk balanced on his knees, tipping precariously from side to side. Around him, nine-year-olds chewed their pencils and bent over their work. The teacher's grimacing and gesticulating became a cartoon with the sound turned off. The sloppily done and missing homework papers, the quizzes with their glaring red *F*'s, grew legs and paraded past him.

"In fact," Dan continued, "they say you haven't been doing much of anything."

Michele turned her pale, mournful face toward him. "We just wondered what's troubling you, Cory," she said. "If there's anything we're doing, or aren't doing, that's making you unhappy."

The book she had been reading lay facedown beside her. Cory read the title along the spine: *Childbirth the Natural Way.* No, there was nothing they could do or shouldn't do. It had to do with belonging, and he couldn't belong. He would always be an outsider. He shook his head and averted his eyes.

"I'm sure you don't want to go through fourth grade again," Dan said.

Now, in Cory's mind, his classmates moved through the year in a revolving door, stepping out and into the fifth grade. Cory alone was trapped within the circle, revolving endlessly, getting bigger and older, until there was no way to squeeze out. Then he became gray and bent and hollow, a relic of himself. He thought of Miss Sybil, smiling and inviting children in to sing while she sprinkled sleeping powder into Dixie cups of lime Kool-Aid.

In his pocket, Cory's fingers found the halvah. He longed to taste its sweetness again.

"I'll try to do better," he said, and memory yawned open to consume him. For a moment he could not remember if he was at the Keppermans', the Nortons', or the Sizemores'. He turned and walked the tightrope line toward his room.

"Cory—"

Cory stopped to hear what Dan would say.

"Let him be," Michele told Dan. "Give him time to think."

"Michele, this is serious. I think we need to deal

with this. Ms. Hanks has been called. She's concerned. The teacher wants a conference, maybe a tutor—"

"I just think we shouldn't press him right now."

Was that hurt in Michele's eyes? In Cory's chest there was a sudden stab of pain. Would Michele and Dan start arguing now because of him? Cory guessed that Michele hated arguments as much as he did. He saw himself and Dan rolling down the hillside together, laughing. There was no laughter in Dan's eyes now, nor in Michele's. And what did it mean that Ms. Hanks had been called? That she thought Michele and Dan weren't taking good care of him? Would Ms. Hanks want him to come talk to her every week, plumbing his mind for buried feelings?

"I'll try to do better," Cory repeated.

Dan's jaw tightened. "One week, Cory. We can stall things with the school for one week. If you don't begin to show a real turnaround in that time, we're going to have to do something about this."

One week. What could he show in one week? It was the end of September, and already school seemed to be rushing past him, with chapters unread and lessons not heard. How could he dazzle Dan and Ms. Hanks and his teacher into believing he had changed, when school was more tedious than ever? No, there would be some round-eyed tutor pressing him in the evening when he should be free. There would be Michele's hurt look and Dan scanning his homework papers. But he didn't say these things. He only nodded at Dan and closed his door behind him.

The house seemed strangely silent. The walls bore down on him. Outside he could hear the voices of children calling to each other in play; they seemed far, far away.

Cory sat down on his bed and looked into his palm, trying to pick out the lines that Carlotta had shown him. This was the heart line, the one that brought pain. This was the head line, cut deeply with unwanted thought. And this was the life line that told of travel.

Travel.

6

It was night when Cory slipped from his bedroom window to the grass below, his backpack slung over his shoulder. He stopped, listening. There had been no sound from Michele and Dan's room for an hour.

It was not long before he was crouching beneath Carlotta's window. He wasn't sure how the old lady would react to his leaving, but he felt he had to tell her. After all, it was she who had read the mysterious prophecy in his palm. If that had not happened, he might not have thought of leaving.

Carlotta had moved the circus poster from her window, but now Cory knew which was hers and did not need it. He peeked in and saw that she was alone and in bed. He wondered briefly if she would tell on him and then dismissed the thought. Someone who secretly made candy in her room, who cursed Miss

46

Sybil and slipped past her watchful eyes, would not tell.

He tapped on the window with his fingertips and hunched down. There was no response. He tried again, more loudly. In a moment, Carlotta was peering out at him.

"I'm leaving," he whispered. "I just wanted you to know."

Her dark eyes grew round. "Where?"

In a flash of realization, Cory saw her as that fierce, caged lion—Zeba—of which she had spoken. Pacing, longing to be free, but always under Miss Sybil's fleshy, grasping hand. He wanted to free her. "I don't know," he answered, "but you can come with me if you want to."

Carlotta jerked back and grasped the window ledge with two thin hands. Cory wondered if the circus animals were startled by the jerking open of their cage doors, by the vision of freedom that lay suddenly before them.

"I—I am an old woman," she faltered.

"You don't have to come. I mean, I'll understand if you don't. But I just thought you didn't belong here."

She stared. Cory thought he could see himself reflected in her eyes, shining in the dark spheres. He glanced around the vacant yard. Staying there was making him nervous; Miss Sybil was sure to discover him.

"Can you get out?" he asked.

"I can get out," Carlotta said slowly.

"Then will you meet me in the woods?"

"I will meet you."

Cory took time for a quick grin in reply, then stole through the shadows along the building. At the end of the wing, he darted across the lawn into the woods. Through the filtered moonlight he made his way to the fallen tree and settled down against it to wait.

At first he expected to see her slight, ghostly form following right behind him. But she did not come and did not come, and his eyelids grew heavy with sleepiness. He wondered if she had changed her mind. And he grew impatient with himself—what was he thinking of, asking an old lady like that to run away with him? She would surely slow him down.

He had had no choice but to ask her. They were family now. Even their palms were alike, she had said.

Two hours passed before Carlotta roused him. Cory rubbed the sleep from his eyes and wondered, for a moment, why they were there.

"It took me a long while to get out," explained Carlotta. "I had to wait for Sybil to sleep and for the night nurse to be busy." She pulled her flowered carpetbag to her. "I was all packed. I am always packed. We stayed packed in the circus."

"I was afraid you wouldn't hear me," Cory told her. "I was afraid they gave you sleeping pills."

"They do." Carlotta smiled. "I put them in the toilet."

———

The Greyhound station had a sad weariness to it. Two broken-down men sat outside, sharing drinks from a bottle in a brown paper bag. Inside, another man dozed on the hard, dark bench. Everything seemed filmed with a layer of dust.

Carlotta sat on the bench, worn out from their walk. She listened as Cory read the bus schedule. A bus was leaving soon for Lanton, a city one hundred fifty miles away, across the state line. Cory had never been there. They would not be noticed in the city, Carlotta pointed out. And it would probably be easier for them to get by.

Cory spoke with the ticket man and reported that Carlotta's ticket would cost $25.55 and his $12.78.

"You have money?" Carlotta asked.

"Yeah. Thirty-six fifty I've saved from my dinky allowance and from doing yard work."

Carlotta looked quickly around. "Do not talk about what you have so that others might hear. And do not flash your money about." Furtively, she drew three well-worn tens from a tin box inside her bag and handed them to Cory to buy her ticket.

Cory boarded the bus with relief. Neither the ticket seller nor the driver thought there was anything strange about them. He had been afraid they might take one look at them and think, "runaways." They probably would have if he was traveling alone in the middle of the night, he realized. Because of Carlotta, they were not suspicious.

He looked beyond Carlotta to the darkness rolling past their window. It was as if nothing were there; as if they and their handful of fellow passengers were all there were in the world, riding in a dimly lit capsule rumbling through a great black emptiness.

He wondered what Michele and Dan would think when they discovered he was gone. They would probably be relieved that they would not have to explain to him that they were going to have a baby and had to send him back to the children's shelter. Maybe they would start fixing up his room for the baby. They wouldn't have to deal with his school problems or worry when he was late.

And what about Ms. Hanks? Would she cross him off her caseload, glad that she wouldn't need to worry about finding him another place to live, about figuring out what was wrong with him? Would she put some other kid in his place to sing with Alonso, Erica, and Robert?

"What's going to happen when they find out you're gone?" he asked Carlotta.

"Probably they will call the police," she said in a low voice. "They will announce it on television: 'An elderly woman apparently wandered away from Miss Sybil's Shady Rest.' Always they say old people 'wander away.' They never think old people can decide to go someplace. They will say, 'Last seen she was wearing a blue nightgown.'" She smiled.

Cory grinned, too, at the picture of Carlotta wandering aimlessly about town in a nightgown. "Do you suppose they'll figure we left together?"

She shrugged. "It is not likely. Miss Sybil will carry on as if she is worried to death about me, the old prune."

Cory settled into the padded seat, tipping the back down to a reclining position. He felt like he'd been awake forever. "I bet Michele and Dan will, too. And Ms. Hanks." It was a pleasant sort of feeling to think of them all wringing their hands and worrying about him, while he sped off to new adventures, a new life. No school, no tutor, no Foster Friends Club, no shifting about from home to home, never quite fitting in. He couldn't be deserted if he left first.

"I thought you liked those people."

"They're okay, I guess. But they're gonna have a kid of their own. They don't want me hanging around." He was angry at the lump that rose in his throat. He turned to his side as best he could in the slanted plush seat. "I'm going to sleep," he announced. "I'm beat."

Cory awoke with difficulty. Dimly he perceived that the motion that had lulled him to sleep had stopped, but sleepiness still enfolded him like a fog. The bus driver gently shook him, and Cory looked up, blinking.

"Come on, son," said the driver. "Better wake Grandma up. This is your stop."

Cory turned to Carlotta, who snored softly, chin on chest. He nudged her. "Wake up, Grandma," he said. "This is Lanton."

Bleary-eyed and achy from sleeping in bus seats, they gathered their things and walked down the aisle. They were the last ones on the bus.

Outside, dawn was streaking fingers of light into the sky. Cory drank in the moist, cool air.

"What did you call me on the bus?" Carlotta asked.

"Grandma." Cory flushed. "The driver called you that, so I thought I'd better."

She nodded. "It is a good idea. You must call me Grandma whenever we are in public, so people will not be suspicious."

She shifted her bag to the other hand. Cory noticed she seemed more bent over than he'd seen her before. Probably her back was stiff from not sleeping in a bed. He reached out to take her bag. "Want me to carry that?"

She moved the bag out of his reach. "I can carry my own weight," she said. "I always have."

Cory adjusted the pack on his back and shoved his hands into his pockets. Now what, he wondered. Now we're in Lanton, what do we do? All his thoughts had been on leaving. He had not stopped to consider arriving.

Carlotta was walking toward town as if she knew where she was headed.

"Where're you going, Carlotta?" he asked. "What d'you think we should do?"

"We will need a place to live, unless you brought a tent—and you cannot pitch a tent in the city. You do not want to sleep under a bridge, do you?"

"No."

"Well, then, we must get a room, and we have precious little money, so it will not be anything fancy."

Cory felt irritated that she had thought of this before him. After all, running away had been his idea. "Do you think we can find anything this early in the morning?"

She stopped short. "No. I guess not."

Cory felt more generous again, since she had conceded a point to him. "There's a park over there," he said. "Why don't we sit and rest awhile."

As they sat on the park bench Cory gazed at the smokestacks rising on the horizon. The grayness of the city seemed to come from more than the fading darkness. Lanton was a far cry from the modest white houses and the trim green lawns of the town they'd left.

If Cory had imagined arriving at all, it was with excitement and the anticipation of freedom. Instead, he felt like he'd been pummeled. There were aches in parts of his back he had never thought of before. He hadn't had much sleep, and his stomach had begun to grumble in anticipation of a breakfast he hadn't planned for. He announced this to Carlotta.

She pulled out a plastic bag of halvah and broke off a piece for each of them. "This is all that is left," she said.

"How come Miss Sybil didn't want you to make this stuff?" Cory asked, biting into it.

"We do not do things for ourselves at Miss Sybil's. Others do for us. I did not want her to know because she would call it making a mess." Carlotta's mouth had become a thin, unhappy line.

"Sounds terrible there," said Cory. "She didn't act too happy about you having money, either."

"If she knew I had saved this little bit, she would take it to pay for my staying there. She would like to see me penniless."

Cory wondered how much Carlotta had in that tin box, but he didn't dare ask.

The sky was now painted in pale shades of pink and yellow, but Cory could not see the sun for all the buildings. A garbage truck rattled by, two men hanging on its rear. Lights were on in the diner opposite the park, and a few people were beginning to appear on the streets.

Cory yawned and stretched. He thought of how nice it would be to order a plate of bacon and eggs and a cup of cocoa. He wondered how much it would cost.

They sat numbly watching as awnings were unrolled and OPEN signs posted. People passed by them without a glance.

Everyone else in Lanton seems to know where they're going, thought Cory.

Finally, Carlotta stood up. "It is time we find a room."

7

"I ain't got but one bed," Mr. Grizowski said. "But I can rent you a rollaway for the boy."

The landlord smelled of stale tobacco, and his striped sweater, Cory thought, made him look like a high school kid wearing an old-man mask.

Cory stepped out of the dark hallway and into the room. They'd been walking for hours, newspaper in hand, trying to find their way around the foreign streets of Lanton. His shoulders ached from the weight of his pack, and his stomach was complaining again. This was the fifth place they'd looked at. The first place housed only men, although the newspaper ad hadn't bothered to say so. The second cost thirty dollars a week, which Carlotta said was too much. There was another place where the landlady asked pointed questions about them and what they were doing in Lanton. She wanted references and to know their source of money. They didn't even see that room. And at the last one, Cory had been chilled by the sudden silence and watchful eyes of the men loitering in the hallway.

They had just happened to pass by this building, an old row house. Cory noticed the small rectangular sign on the door that read simply ROOM. He almost didn't care what the room looked like. It was quiet, and there was no one in the hall. Besides, he was tired of walking.

The room looked tired and used, too. The faded wallpaper showed ladies in huge skirts and men in powdered wigs. The heavy green curtains looked grimy. There were cigarette burns on the dresser top.

"The rollaway is how much?" asked Carlotta. She was breathless from her climb up the steep stairway.

"Eight dollars a week." He looked critically at Cory. "'Course we don't have no kids here. We couldn't have a lot of noise or writin' on the walls."

"I don't write on walls." Cory was disgusted.

"Eight is too much," said Carlotta. She started toward the door.

"I could sleep on the floor," Cory offered. Anything but more searching, he thought, but Carlotta was not listening to him.

"Well, I could make it five, if you don't tell no one," Mr. Grizowski conceded.

"You have a kitchen and a bathroom?"

Cory sat on the edge of the easy chair, examining a hole in the upholstery. Mr. Grizowski cast a nervous look at him. He seemed anxious to have them move along. "Kitchen and bathroom to share, yes, ma'am. Down the hall here."

They peered into the bathroom, where the tub stood on four little legs with a gray curtain sagging above it. In the kitchen there was a gas stove, a refrigerator, a sink, and a scarred table. The man showed them the section of cupboard where they could keep their food.

Carlotta turned her back on the man and slipped some bills out of her tin box. "Twenty-five dollars," she said, counting the money into his hand.

The man grunted in acknowledgment, folding the money into a little square that he put into his pocket. "Rent due every Monday. I'll bring that rollaway."

It was a crummy place, Cory admitted to himself later, as he was putting his things in his half of the dresser. Not just old, like the Keppermans', but old and battered. Still, it was theirs. Having repaid Carlotta for his half of the rent, he felt a certain pride of ownership.

Carlotta had taken off her shoes and lain down on the big bed, her long, full skirt spread out like a fan.

Cory wondered what the morning had been like

for Michele and Dan. Michele would have called him to breakfast, tentatively knocking on his door when he didn't come right away. He tried to imagine her face when she discovered his bed unslept in. Dan probably went out to search the neighborhood for him. Was he angry? Or maybe he'd just gone on to work. Now Michele could work full-time again—until the baby.

"I traveled, just like you read in my palm I would," he said.

"Yes. This morning in the park I saw a grasshopper. This means travel and good fortune."

"Tell me about when you were with the circus, Carlotta."

A little puff of sound escaped her, and Cory waited. "When I was sixteen, I saw Philo's circus. It was the first circus I had ever seen." There was a silence in which Cory settled himself cross-legged on the rollaway bed. A large, dark water bug skittered across the floor and disappeared. Then Carlotta spoke again, her voice low and soothing. "I thought this was the most beautiful thing in the world. The costumes flashing like colored stars, the animals so strong and wild. Only later did I understand how trapped they were, and how faded the stars. My mama and papa, they worked in the shoe factory and me also, after school. Mama says I should quit school and work all day there. Papa is not sure. He wants an education for me. They argue and I leave to settle it. That was the beginning." Her voice had grown so soft that

Cory had to strain to hear it. "I am tired now, Cory. I must rest."

"Okay." He lay back on the rollaway and looked at the crack in the ceiling, zigzagging like lightning. To himself, he repeated his new name for Carlotta: Grandma. He liked the sound of it. There had never been a grandmother in his life. His parents had never spoken of one. Now he had found himself a grandma. In the whole world, she had no one but him. And he had no one but her.

The room seemed to tip and revolve, and Cory knew that sleep was coming. He lay one arm up over his head and gave in to it.

"So I spent three dollars and five cents—what's the big deal? You're hungry, aren't you?" Cory was angry. He thought she'd be pleased that he'd gone out and bought them lunch. All they'd had that day was halvah.

Carlotta glared at the bag he'd set on her bed. "You call this food? Greasy meat? Coca-Cola?"

"What's wrong with cheeseburgers and Cokes? And I got a large bag of fries instead of two small ones, 'cause that was cheaper. I saved thirty-seven cents." He felt wounded that she did not appreciate this thrifty decision.

"How much do you think you could get at the market for that money? Probably enough for a package of cheese, a carton of milk, and a whole loaf of bread."

"Well, you don't *have* to eat it. I bought it with my money, anyway," he grumbled.

"Your money, my money, what is the difference?" she demanded. "When you do not have the rent, then do you go sleep under the bridge? No—I help you."

"Well, you don't *have* to," he said stiffly. "I can take care of myself."

She snatched up her carpetbag and stomped out into the hall. A moment later, Cory heard the shower running. He unwrapped one of the cheeseburgers and took a bite. In his mouth, it turned to sawdust. He didn't even feel hungry now. He sat on the window-sill, looking out at the city. It looked gray and un-friendly. He thought of the six dollars he had left in his pocket. Carlotta was right. The money would go fast. And then what *would* he do?

He went downstairs and knocked on the land-lord's door. The old man opened the door a crack and peered out at him. "Yeah?"

"I, uh, wondered if you had some work for me to do. You know, cutting the lawn or washing the windows?"

The man grunted. "Ain't hardly lawns in the city, boy. You trying to get your money back, huh? Well, I do the work myself, see. That way I keep the money in *my* pocket."

Cory mounted the steps slowly. When he opened the door to their room, Carlotta was sitting on the bed, combing out her damp hair. She looked at him briefly. "Come in. We will eat lunch and then we will think what to do."

Looking for work was a tiring enterprise. Just descending the steps of their building made Carlotta breathless and weak in the legs, and Cory wondered if they should have held out for a first-floor room. He worried, too, whether there was some medicine she was supposed to be taking and did not have, but she insisted not.

At a drugstore they read over the help wanted section in the newspaper until the store manager asked them pointedly if they'd like to buy it. "No, thank you," Carlotta told him crisply, and they left. No one seemed to be looking for an eleven-year-old boy or a seventy-five-year-old woman, anyway.

"I will not be a beggar," Carlotta informed him as they stopped to eat a slice each of the day-old bread Carlotta had purchased. "Some can stand on a corner and beg, but always I have earned my keep. I will also not steal."

Cory considered these possibilities for himself. He did not enjoy the plain, slightly stale bread, and what if their money ran out? Then what? If begging or stealing meant that he and Carlotta would eat, he thought perhaps he could do it. But one look at her set, closed-up expression discouraged him from telling her so.

"You know, I bet we could find an abandoned

house and live there," Cory suggested. "It would save us twenty-five dollars a week."

"You are in the city, Cory," Carlotta reminded him. "Abandoned buildings are homes for drunks and thieves. Even if they were not, there could be no light at night—it would bring the police."

Cory bit the center out of a folded piece of bread and opened it up to inspect the hole.

They spent several days scrounging Lanton for work. The streets looked more dingy and dirty to Cory each day they walked them. Cory answered an ad for a messenger boy, but he was told that the "boy" they had in mind had to be at least eighteen and out of high school. Carlotta answered an ad for a baby-sitter/housekeeper and was told that it was a live-in job. Taking in an eleven-year-old boy as well was not part of the employer's plan.

Each day they bought something different from the market. This was Carlotta's idea. Over the course of a week, she explained, they would have a balanced diet. The food would not have a chance to spoil, and they would not have to spend a lot at once. They had a bread day, a day of carrots, a day of apples. Cory's legs felt shaky and tired. Carlotta seemed to be slowing down, too. He thought of Michele's neat line of cookbooks on the kitchen shelf. She was methodically working her way through them. They were up to roast leg of lamb when he left—with Dan's discount at the grocery, Michele said they could try most any kind of meat they wanted. Cory had been looking forward to shish kebabs, which Michele said they would make together on the grill outside. Were they making shish kebabs without him tonight? And then there were the cookies—the last batch was orange marmalade drops.

"We will have cheese tomorrow," Carlotta promised. "The protein will make you feel better."

"When do we get a pie day or a candy bar day?"

"When you have only a little to eat," Carlotta said, "you must eat what will make you healthy."

"What happens when we run out of money?" Cory wanted to know.

"There are places where people can get a free meal. Salvation Army, they call it."

Cory stopped eating his apple in midbite. "There are? Why didn't you say so!"

Expressionless, Carlotta said simply, "It is like begging, to go there."

Cory looked away. A big free meal was waiting for them somewhere in Lanton, and Carlotta was too stubborn to get it! In his frustration, he felt like pitching his half-eaten apple across the street. Instead, he took another bite. He was too hungry to part with it. Then Cory saw a rumpled-looking man in a winter jacket and hat and carrying a crushed sack cut through the park where they sat.

"It's not that cold. Why is he wearing a winter coat?" Cory asked Carlotta.

"Because he has no place to hang it," Carlotta said softly. "He has no home."

Cory watched as the man picked through a trash can, retrieving a half-eaten hamburger from a piece of foil. He wondered if Carlotta would help him find the Salvation Army kitchen before they had to do that.

"Where is your mother, Cory?" Carlotta asked suddenly.

Cory felt a little prickly warning sensation. "I don't know. She didn't exactly leave me her card, you know. What has she got to do with anything?"

Carlotta glanced at him. "I guess nothing. I am an old woman, Cory. Who will hire me? I have not worked in years. Maybe I am too old to work."

"Did you go right from the circus to Miss Sybil's?"

"No. I had a room and put out a sign for fortune-teller. I also served in a Salvation Army kitchen—a place to eat for the unshaven men and the faded women. A parade of the lost."

That was why Carlotta didn't want to go to the free-meal place, Cory thought. It meant they'd be lost, defeated. But that was still better than eating from the garbage can.

"What about this foster mother," Carlotta continued. "What was her name?"

"Michele. But she's not a real mother. She's only twenty-four. What does she want with a kid eleven years old?" Now Carlotta was trying to figure out what to do with him. Why did everyone consider him such a problem—his mother; Ms. Hanks; all those

---

64

foster parents, Michele and Dan included; teachers. Well, he had news for every last one: They didn't have to worry about Cory Wainwright. He could take care of himself. "Hey, if you think you're going to get me to go back there, you're crazy. You go back, if you want to, but I'm not. I'll make out somehow," he added.

Cory got up to check the coin return in the telephone near where they had stopped. He'd been checking all the telephones and drink machines along the way. So far he had found a nickel in a soda machine and three cents in the street.

He reached into the little silver hollow. "Bingo!" he cried. He turned and triumphantly held up the quarter for Carlotta to see.

"There is good fortune." Carlotta stood up, shifting the weight of the carpetbag in her hands. She would not leave it in their room, afraid someone would steal it. "Now we will go into this restaurant and get a drink," she announced.

He looked at her in surprise. "Don't you want me to get us something from the market? Wouldn't that be cheaper?"

"It would be cheaper," she admitted. "But sometimes we must spend for the sake of our spirits. I am tired, and I want to sit in a warm place and drink coffee."

Cory did not need to be persuaded. He was tired, too. Somehow, he decided, the money problem would take care of itself. Who knows? Cory thought. They might find a twenty-dollar bill that had fallen from the pocket of some long-departed customer in the seat.

"Coffee, black," Carlotta told the waitress.

"I'll have a Coke," said Cory.

"My grandson will have a glass of milk," said Carlotta.

"I didn't ask for milk. I want a Coke."

The waitress drummed her pencil on her order pad.

"A growing boy needs milk," Carlotta said firmly. "It would not do for you to get sick."

"Carlotta—" began Cory, after the waitress was gone.

"Mind your manners, young man," said Carlotta. "It is Grandma to you."

Cory scowled. It seemed to him that Carlotta was pushing this grandmother thing too far. He couldn't see that a glass of milk was going to do anything for his spirit. He considered pointing out that her coffee was not helping her keep strong and healthy but let it pass. Arguing with her in public made him feel like a whiny, begging kid.

His eye fell on a sign advertising home-baked cherry pie. How good that would be, he thought—even with milk. But he'd never talk her out of the money. That was going too far, she'd say. Then another thought struck him.

"Halvah!" he cried.

"What?" The waitress delivered their drinks, and Carlotta pulled her cup of coffee to her.

Cory leaned over, dropping his voice. "What if we sold your halvah to restaurants? They could advertise like on that pie sign."

Carlotta looked at the sign. "You think they would buy?"

"Sure! It would be homemade halvah. It's great stuff, but who do you ever see selling it?"

"We maybe could sell to groceries, too." Carlotta's eyes began to shine with possibilities. "I can also make Hungarian poppy-seed bread." She smiled. It was the first time Cory had seen her smile since they'd arrived in Lanton.

"We can make them in the kitchen at the rooming house, and I can deliver them to our customers."

"I have many recipes," Carlotta said. "Recipes from all over the world. I have them all here." She tapped her forehead. "In the circus, when I worked in the kitchen, I would bake things from the performers' native lands. I would give them a bit of their homes as a present."

"We'll have a bakery!" Cory exulted.

Carlotta took a swallow of coffee. "Finish up," she said. "We have much to do."

8

Carlotta drew in a ragged breath and put down several of their precious dollars on ingredients for their first batch of halvah. They'd have to begin with one product, she told Cory. As it began to make money for them, they'd buy the makings of their next item. Their operation could expand indefinitely, adding more products and more customers.

"We'll hire bakers and salespeople!" Cory cried, and threw his hands into the air. "We'll be rich and go to Florida every winter! We can call it the C & C Bakery—okay?"

She nodded and allowed him to carry the bag of groceries.

In the kitchen, while Carlotta laid out the ingredients on the battered little kitchen table, Cory made a list of things she said they could make. Hungarian poppy-seed bread, Swedish tea ring, Portuguese rice pudding, pashka, baklava, linzertorte—their very names made Cory's mouth water with anticipation. To this list he added one of his own: American cowboy biscuits, which Michele had taught him to make.

After the grinding, the mixing, the cutting, and the wrapping of the halvah, they fell wearily into their beds, their spirits stirred and waiting.

The next morning, Cory awoke to the sound of a truck rumbling down their street. The thick, wavery glass rattled in the window frames. In the distance he heard the morning whistle of one of the factories. Cory stretched and lay still a moment. Beneath his back he felt dips in the mattress where it folded. He wondered what it would be like to be folded up in the rollaway, bent in sharp, strange angles and pressed against the thick, soft mattress. Then he remembered the halvah and got up.

Carlotta was still sleeping, her face blurred and brown against the stark white sheets. Cory hesitated and then shook her shoulder gingerly. It startled him, how twiglike she felt; it was as if she might snap in two if he gripped her too hard. "It's morning," he said. "We need to sell the halvah."

Her eyes snapped open. She took a moment to bring him into focus. "Halvah," she repeated.

"Yeah. We have to take it to the stores today. I'll, um, see you in the kitchen." He fished his last clean set of clothes from the dresser drawer and headed for the bathroom.

Later, when Carlotta came into the kitchen, he was sorry he'd awakened her. Her shoulders sagged. She seemed bruised rather than refreshed by the sleep.

"You okay?"

"Of course." Without looking at him, she went to the cupboard and withdrew a chipped china bowl. She placed the plastic-wrapped squares of halvah in it one at a time.

"Sit down and have breakfast first," said Cory. "It's cheese day."

She accepted the chunk he held out and sat. When he produced an apple saved from yesterday, she almost smiled. Their diet was harder on her than she let on, he realized. "When we sell our halvah," he said, "I'm taking you out for a steak dinner. French fries, beans, everything."

She touched his cheek with three cool, narrow fingers and turned away. "We had better go then."

The first place they stopped was an expensive-looking restaurant. Stiff cloth napkins stood like little tents on the tables. The upside-down water glasses reflected the light of the chandeliers. They would have plenty of money to buy halvah, Cory thought.

But the manager declined to even taste it. He was tall and round. Carlotta seemed to shrink before him. "We make all of our own desserts on the premises," the manager announced, gazing over their heads.

You wouldn't have to, Cory thought. You could

just try it. But he felt himself growing smaller, his throat closing up, and he said nothing.

Outside the restaurant he was angry with himself. "I should have said something," he fumed. "I could have said *something*, at least. I hate rich people."

Carlotta pursed her lips but did not answer.

At the next restaurant, Cory tried harder.

"I don't know," said the manager, a woman with several chins. "We don't usually buy from private folks."

Cory lifted his chin. "Why don't you try a piece anyway, ma'am. We live real near here. Won't be any problem getting it to you."

She hesitated and then picked a square from the bowl Carlotta held. Cory watched her chins wobble as she chewed. "I can bring you a batch tomorrow, if you want," he offered.

"It is tasty," the woman admitted. "Let me think on it. I'll talk to my sister. Come back another time, hear?"

"She didn't say no," Cory said, after the restaurant door swung shut behind them.

"She did not say yes."

"Carlotta, I think I can do this."

"What?"

"Sell the halvah. You're tired. Why don't you rest in the park, and I'll take the halvah around."

"I—"

"Let me see if I can do it, Carlotta."

Her eyes flickered over him, and then she smiled. "All right. I will wait for you. At the bench by the fountain."

Cory took the bowl from her and headed for the restaurant where he'd seen the home-baked pie sign.

"Your grandmother, huh," said the manager, as she chewed on a piece of halvah. "I saw you two in here yesterday, didn't I?"

"Yes, ma'am. I saw your pie sign and—"

"She looked pretty old. You sure she's up to all that baking?"

"It's no baking to it, really. Just mixing. And she loves to do it."

"Wouldn't do to have a sign up for this stuff and then run out of it."

Cory's fingers, tightening on the bowl, were nearly as white as the china. "Oh, no. That's no problem. I help her, and we live close. I can run it down anytime."

"And we might have to have some samples to give away. People don't know what this stuff—halvah?—is. Can you give us some extra?"

Cory considered. "Yes, sure. We can do that till it catches on."

She placed an order.

Cory burst out the door, clutching the receipt slip with the order scrawled across it. He felt like throwing up his hands for joy. Instead, he went to a tiny grocery and a drugstore and took orders there.

"Menkel's Grocery and the Cosy Inn Restaurant have already ordered," he told the pharmacist. "This stuff is becoming really popular, and I thought you might want to stock it."

Now he ran to the park, holding the bowl with its bouncing candies to his chest. When he reached Carlotta he set the bowl in her lap and dropped the order slips into it.

"I did it! I sold to three places! They love it! We have work, Carlotta!"

"Cory," she said simply, and her look was full of pride. She held the bowl out to him. "Eat, Cory."

The lightness Cory felt in that moment seemed to seep down through several layers. "Don't you want me to go sell more? There's lots more places—"

"Eat, my golden young salesman. It is enough for one day."

And it was all they could handle until they were paid for their wares. After feasting on the remaining halvah, they went back to the rooming house and began making more.

Success had infused Cory with a new energy. As he ground more seeds, he felt eager to talk. "Didn't you ever have any kids?"

"Peter-John had children—and the ticket girl. Three little towheads. They would come to the show sometimes when we performed in New Jersey. They were bored, gangly things the last time I saw them. And then Peter-John stopped bringing them."

"Why didn't you marry Peter-John?"

"I thought life was too full then. The circus was like a family. But for Peter-John, no. He yearned away from it. And me, I thought I would dry up like a prune without it."

"I guess that was a long time ago, back in the olden days," Cory reflected, seeing anew Carlotta's weathered face. There were times when he would think of her as being like himself. Then he would call her Grandma in public or speak with her about the past, and she would slide into focus suddenly, and he would remember.

"A lifetime ago," she replied. "Where are those seeds?"

He dumped the ground seeds into the bowl. "Then you never had any grandchildren."

"No."

"I never had a grandmother, either."

She looked up from mixing, and Cory examined the innards of the grinder for more sesame meal.

"Sybil calls old age golden years. What a silly thing this is. There was nothing golden at that place. The black years, I call them. There is nothing golden about bedpans and sleeping pills. But *these* days, Cory, *these* days I call golden."

Cory glanced up quickly. Her look was so tender that Cory had to turn away. "I'll wrap the halvah when it's mixed," he said huskily. "You can rest."

The days passed this way, Carlotta preparing larger batches and Cory running deliveries. Each day he took a portion of the halvah as samples and tried to find new customers. With some of this profit, they bought Cory a pair of secondhand sneakers at a thrift shop, and Cory dumped the old, battered ones in the wastebasket. Their meals became more normal, and they even splurged on a pound of bacon. Carlotta wrote their initials on the package—C & C—so that the other roomers would not eat it. Each night they had bacon, lettuce, and tomato sandwiches for supper.

"Maybe we should rename it Grasshopper Bakery," Cory suggested, "for the grasshopper you saw that brought us good luck."

Carlotta smiled.

But their troubles were not over. Sometimes Carlotta thought some of the halvah was missing in the morning when Cory packed it in a bag for delivery. The halvah could be kept in their room. But the bacon could not, and it, too, had been disappearing faster than they used it.

She suspected Eleanor, the sewing machine operator with the missing forefinger who lived down the hall. Several mornings before Eleanor left for work, the unmistakable aroma of bacon drifted down the hall to their room.

Finally, Carlotta confronted her.

"Who knows whose is what, with your stuff everywhere," Eleanor shot back.

"You would know if you bought halvah or a

pound of bacon," Carlotta maintained. "You would know if C & C was written on the package that it was not yours!"

Eleanor shook her middle finger at Carlotta. "You've got a lot of nerve accusing decent, hard-workin' folk, old woman!"

In Cory, a smoldering anger was fanned. "Who are you calling old woman? You just better shut up!"

Eleanor stepped back, nearly upsetting her pot of canned soup on the stove. "Don't you talk nasty to me, Mr. Biggety. I'd like to know why a child your age ain't in school of a day."

Cory and Carlotta finished off the bacon that evening and moved the contents of the cupboard shelf to their dresser top. Some things, of course, had to be left in the refrigerator. But after that, the thieving seemed to stop.

In the evening and on Sundays, they rested. Sometimes the hours seemed to stretch on. Without meaning to, Cory would wonder what Michele and Dan were doing at that moment. He thought of the evenings lounging in front of the television with them. Michele was working on an old-fashioned needlepoint that said Home Sweet Home. She wanted to hang it in the entry hall.

Once they had watched a movie about a woman whose child had been killed by a drunk driver. It took Cory a moment to realize that the muffled noise he heard from Michele was her crying. Why, he wondered. Michele had never had a child. Then Dan drew close to her, cradling her in his arms until she sobbed freely. Such a sudden, fierce pain welled up in Cory then that he had fled to the backyard.

How Carlotta sensed his moody thoughts when he said nothing, Cory didn't know. But she did. She always seemed to pick those moments to pull the scrapbook from its box and, leafing reverently through it, tell Cory stories of the circus. He wondered if she had felt as lost and rootless then, with no parents to love her, as he did now. But the circus was like a family, she'd said, and she had had Peter-John to love her. If he had been Peter-John, he would never have left her. At times he ached for a way to tell her how alike he felt they were, how no blood grandmother could have been closer to him. But these thoughts remained unspoken.

When Cory could bear inactivity no longer, they would walk to the park. There Cory would toss his jacket on a bench and do cartwheels and somersaults, imagining himself to be Anatole of the Flying Trapeze. These were the best times, and Cory thought Carlotta even seemed younger than she had at Miss Sybil's. Under her attentive gaze, Cory felt warmed and cared for, and when he coaxed a smile or laughter from her, it was like a gift shared between them.

One Sunday, though, Carlotta made him put on his best jeans and T-shirt and walk with her the three blocks to the Catholic church.

"Why do we have to go to church?" Cory asked Carlotta. His mother had never taken him to church.

Mrs. Sizemore had, though. She told him to take all his troubles to the Lord. That was just because she didn't want to be bothered with them, he soon decided. He had tried to tell Mrs. Sizemore about the things that had gone wrong in his life. But she had no time to listen—or didn't want to. It was less painful not to start talking, Cory found, than to start and be stopped.

Carlotta fussed with the belt of her swirling lavender skirt as they walked along and then drew her sweater tightly around her. "I would do the same for any grandson," she answered.

Cory sighed. "I didn't even know you were Catholic."

"My family was Catholic."

"I never liked church," he grumbled. But her mouth was set in the firm line that told him her mind was made up, and he said no more.

When they stepped into the sanctuary, Cory sucked in his breath, stopping involuntarily. The high, peaked ceiling seemed to diminish him. Tall narrow windows of mottled glass cast a pale, lemony light over the rows of pews. Carlotta nudged him forward and to a seat.

The worshippers were still filing in. Factory workers, looking scrubbed and splashed awake, laid square hands on the ends of the pews as they knelt quickly before the statue of the Holy Mother. Children crossed themselves with soft, birdlike hands before scrambling to their seats. Mothers knelt praying in the pews with clasped hands, eyes hopeful and distant.

Then a hush fell over the room. The somber, medieval strains of an organ seemed to roll down from on high, filling the church so full that Cory felt he could touch the music. It made him feel dizzy. Everyone rose as down the center aisle came a procession: two priests holding aloft a gold-and-white book and a silver Jesus on a golden cross. They were followed by three altar boys, no older than Cory, in hooded white robes. They looked like small monks.

When the group reached the front, the priest began to pray. His priest's words of sin and forgiveness rang out over the sanctuary and settled like a cloak about Cory's shoulders. "Forgive us, O Lord, where we have fallen short and sinned against you and against our neighbors." Cory's eyes traveled around the church to the statue of Mary. She looked soft and gentle in her flowing gown, with four rows of small candles flickering like stars at her feet. On the far side of the altar stood Joseph, bearded and robed, a kindly man. And between them, high above, was Jesus, nailed to the cross. Achingly thin, mightily alone, his head hung limply on his shoulder. Looking at him gave Cory a stretched, pained feeling.

They sat and the priest talked on. Little boys began to sag against their mothers. The microphone crackled. The priest's voice faded and then rose again. He told of the prodigal son, who took his share of his father's wealth and left home. He squandered the money, but when he came home repentant, his father rejoiced. Who was there, Cory wondered, to rejoice at *his* homecoming? Not his parents, who had left *him*. Not Michele and Dan, busy with the coming of their baby.

Cory and Carlotta rose to pray and sat as the others did throughout the service. Out of the corner of his eye, Cory saw Carlotta struggling to her feet for the third time, her whitening knuckles gripping the back of the pew. She wore a look of irritation.

Then there was a new stirring, and the priests and deacons descended the aisles bearing golden chalices. People were beginning to leave the pews and form lines in the aisles. Cory looked questioningly at Carlotta.

"Communion," she said, and did not move.

Cory watched as the people approached the priest. He fed them each a wafer from his own hand, whispering soothing words that Cory could not hear. The priest seemed to take them in with his eyes, smiling faintly, blessing, feeding. . . . Cory felt his muscles tense as he watched. In his mind's eye he saw Carlotta offering him halvah. And then his mother, slowly, deliberately laying out the jars of peanut butter and Marshmallow Fluff, carefully avoiding his eyes.

Cory's heart was pounding. He wanted to run from the church. Even more, he ached to push his way to the front of the line to be blessed, to be fed from the priest's hand. He imagined the priest touching his head, giving him some special words, words he could hold on to like a talisman to carry him through the length of his days. Carlotta laid a quieting hand on his arm. Startled, Cory glanced at her. Did she see his turmoil? But her gaze was far away. He sank back against the wooden bench. In a moment, she withdrew her hand.

Cory left the church feeling wrung out. The breeze that greeted them as they stepped through the arched doorway was cleansing. With each step toward home, he felt he was leaving troublesome emotions behind. "I don't want to go back there," he told Carlotta.

"We will not go again." Carlotta herself looked worn. "I said I would make the poppy-seed bread today, but I am so tired I do not think I can do it."

They sat down on a park bench so Carlotta could catch her breath before they went on.

"I'll help with the bread if you want to make it later," Cory offered.

She nodded. "We must think of school for you soon, Cory."

"School! Why bring that in? Everything's going fine without it!"

"I make a poor grandmama. I did not even think of school until that Eleanor mentioned it. I have been too busy enjoying your company to think of what you needed."

"I don't need it—I hate it!"

"What grade are you in?"

"I should be in sixth, but—"

"Then that is where we will put you. We will go tomorrow."

"Listen, Carlotta, you can't. They'll want my records from the other school. They'll want to know all about me. Besides, how can I deliver the halvah and the bread? How can I get us new customers?"

"You will deliver in the morning, before school. Or in the afternoon. And I will tell them something about your records. I will tell them they burned."

"I didn't run away for this!" he complained.

"You are a boy. You must do the things boys do."

"Well, maybe I don't like those things," Cory declared. Carlotta was as stubborn as he was, he fumed. Hadn't he run away partly because school was so awful? Was it going to start all over again—the complaining teachers, the kids who let him know he was an outsider? And would she, his only friend in the world, next start bugging him about homework and grades? "You're carrying this grandmother thing too far!" he said.

"You are firing me as a grandmother? We are no longer family?"

They glared at each other, hands on hips. Then Cory shook his head and looked away. "Aw, I don't mean all that," he conceded, slipping his hands into his pockets.

"A grandmother would not let you run wild. If we are family, then I must treat you as family."

9

In the deep, mingled smells of the kitchen, Cory thought he'd made his own homecoming. Reverently, Carlotta drew the two horseshoe loaves of Hungarian poppy-seed bread from the oven and set them to cool on the kitchen table. Warm and brown, they held the sweet promise of sugarplum filling. And so Cory imagined this kitchen and Carlotta—and even himself—full of sweet promise.

Carlotta pushed her thick hair back from her face with a forearm and sank onto the chair.

"Want a glass of cold water, Carlotta?" Cory asked.

She nodded.

He poured the water and, as he was handing it to her, saw Mr. Grizowski in the doorway.

"Cop stopped by the other day," Mr. Grizowski announced.

Cory felt a little warning tingle go through him. Carlotta straightened in her chair and looked at the old man sharply.

Mr. Grizowski pulled a cigarette from the pack of Camels in his sweater pocket and flicked his lighter to it. He waited until he had sucked at the cigarette, emitting a gray cloud of smoke from his mouth and nose, to continue. "Said he'd seen the boy going in and out during the day. Wondered why he wasn't in school. It does seem a curious thing."

"We planned to register him this week," Carlotta said. "We were trying to get settled."

"Seems to me you'da been settled," said Mr. Grizowski. "You two ain't in trouble, are ya? We don't want no trouble with the law here."

"We are not in any trouble."

Cory glanced quickly at Carlotta; her voice had seemed to tremble.

Mr. Grizowski gazed at them a moment, allowed the ash from his cigarette to fall to the floor, and nodded. "You're going to be doing a lot of baking, I'll have to charge you an extra two dollars for the gas."

"That will not be necessary," said Carlotta.

Mr. Grizowski grunted and turned to go. He looked back over his shoulder. "Seems a curious thing for a boy to call his grandmother 'Carlotta.' "

Neither of them said a word until they heard the landlord descend the stairs.

Then Carlotta said, "What food do we have left in the refrigerator, Cory?" She began wrapping the loaves of poppy-seed bread in foil.

Cory poked around the refrigerator. "Just half a lettuce and a couple pieces of bacon." They had let the food run low in order to pay the rent and buy the bread ingredients.

"Leave it, then. It will only spoil. Get a bag for the bread."

Cory took a paper bag from beneath the sink and began packing the bread. "What are we going to do?"

"Leave Lanton."

"You think that cop will come back?"

"He was not asking questions for no reason."

They hurried to the room and packed their bags without speaking. Cory's stomach knotted up. Could they be arrested for something? He was just a kid. What could they do but send him back to the children's shelter? But Carlotta. Could they arrest her?

"You go now," said Carlotta. "Go to the bus station."

"What about you?"

"I will come, but after."

"I don't think I should leave without you." What if the police officer returned, he wondered. What if she fell down the stairs? Cory couldn't help but feel something terrible might happen if he left her alone.

"If we leave together," Carlotta reasoned, "he will think we are running because of what he said. He may call the police. We go separately, so he is not suspicious."

"Well, let me take the bread, then. He'll see me going off like I always do, making deliveries." Mr. Grizowski probably knew nothing of their baking business, Cory realized. But at least it persuaded Carlotta to hand over the bag so she had only her bulging carpetbag to deal with.

"You won't be long?" he questioned, before opening the door.

"I will watch you from the window. Then I will come quickly. You read the schedule. Pick out a nice new home for us."

Laden with his overstuffed backpack and the bag of groceries, Cory felt conspicuous as he made his way down the steps of their building. This was not the way he looked when he left to make deliveries. He felt as if a dozen pairs of eyes were watching him between parted blinds, wondering what he was up to.

At the bus station, he scanned the schedule nervously. There was a bus leaving soon for a town called Hurley, two hours away. Hurley. Cory liked the sound of that—round and full, like something thrown into space, spinning. It seemed to fit them. He started toward the ticket counter and stopped. If Carlotta shouldn't come in time, the money would be gone. If something happened to her . . .

He strode to the door and saw Carlotta down the street. Her slight frame was bent to one side to offset the weight of the carpetbag. The bag swung against her leg as she hurried toward the station, making her seem to hobble.

I love her, Cory thought suddenly. She's my grandmother and I love her. The thought rocked him. He could not remember ever feeling this sudden shock of love. It was almost painful, but it was a sweet pain. He knew he must have a grandmother or two somewhere. But he knew nothing of them, felt nothing for them. A grandmother you chose, though, was special. Even sacred. Like the holy book the priest held aloft, Cory felt he must keep Carlotta apart and special in his mind.

He tossed his bags on the bench and ran to meet her.

"You have found us a home?" she asked.

"Yes," he said, taking her bag. "Hurley. Don't worry, Grandma. Everything's going to be fine."

She smiled and wrapped her arm around his.

The bus was nearly empty. Cory and Carlotta settled themselves in the back, and once more Cory felt that they were in a world belonging only to themselves. This time, though, they were traveling by day. The scenery passed by in flashes of light. The smoke from their exhaust puffed up like a dusty curtain between them and all they were leaving behind.

Beside him, Carlotta began to hum. The tune touched a memory he could not quite place. Then she began to softly sing, "I am a poor wayfaring stranger—A-trav'ling through—this world of woe—"

Cory joined in. "Yet there's no sickness, toil, or

danger—In that bright world to which I go."

They looked at each other and smiled as if a secret had passed between them. "I thought you did not sing," said Carlotta.

"I thought *you* didn't."

"A bird does not sing in the nighttime. But I feel daylight all around us now, Cory."

"Hurley's going to be great, Carlotta." Contented, he kicked his feet up on the seat in front of him.

When he hopped down from the bus in the town of Hurley a couple of hours later, Cory was sure he had chosen well. The sign he saw posted on the telephone pole proved it. "Look at this!" he cried. "You must have seen another grasshopper!"

Carlotta smiled as she walked toward him. "No grasshopper. What is it?" She squinted at the poster and read the words aloud. "Macklin Brothers Circus."

He felt like turning a cartwheel right there on the pavement. He was as proud as if he had arranged for the circus to be there especially for her. "We can join the circus, Carlotta, just like you did. I'll be the lion tamer. Back, Zeba, back!" He lunged with an imaginary chair at an imaginary lion.

Carlotta did not smile this time. Cory stopped his clowning and took the carpetbag from her. "What's the matter?"

"Oh, Cory. You do not know circus life—"

"Come on. There's a bench. Let's sit down. You okay?"

"Yes, but, Cory, it is a hard—"

"We're tough. We can do it. You hungry?" He pulled a loaf of poppy-seed bread from the bag.

"We need that to sell," Carlotta objected.

"We've got to eat," he pointed out. "You thirsty? Wait here. I'll get us something."

"Some coffee, Cory. Coffee would be wonderful."

Cory trotted off. In a few minutes he returned with a pint of milk for them to share. "Got to keep your strength up," he explained, offering the carton to her for the first swallow. "Coffee doesn't do a thing for you, you know."

Carlotta pursed her lips, and then a chuckle escaped her and she shook her head. "You are as hard-headed as Miss Sybil," she said, and laughed again. "Worse."

"Almost as bad as you." Happy, Cory sat down beside her and broke off a piece of the poppy-seed bread for each of them.

"Plah!" he cried, spitting the bread on the ground. "Is it supposed to taste salty like that?"

"Salty?" Carlotta tasted her piece and then frowned. "This is not the way my bread tastes. It should be sweet. Oh, Cory, have I put in a half-cup of salt and a teaspoon of sugar instead of the other way? Did you see me do that?"

Cory shook his head. "I guess it'd be easy to mix it up when you don't have the recipe written down."

"I do not need a recipe!" Carlotta sounded almost angry. "Always I remember."

There didn't seem to be a satisfactory way to answer this. Cory rewrapped the bread. He wondered if even the birds would eat it.

"All this money spent on cream and candied fruit and honey . . ." Carlotta lamented.

"Do they feed you if you work for the circus?"

Carlotta's gaze shifted back to Cory. "The circus life is hard, Cory. I have not been with the circus for many years. They do not want an old lady like me in the way."

"Is that what your palm says?" Cory took her hand and turned it palm-up, tracing a maze of lines. "I see the Macklin Brothers Circus," he said mysteriously. "I see fame and fortune for you and—yes!—for your grandson, too."

Carlotta withdrew her hand. "All right. We will try."

Eddie Macklin looked down at them from the open door of his trailer. A toothpick flicked on his lip as he spoke. "I don't have much time. What do you want?"

Cory wished the man would step down. Macklin was a big man to begin with, and looking up at him this way made Cory feel even smaller.

"We are looking for work," Carlotta said.

Macklin snorted with amusement. "You're a pair to be running away with the circus!"

Cory defended Carlotta. "My grandmother was a

fortune-teller for years and before that a magician's assistant and—"

This seemed to amuse Macklin all the more. "Fortune-teller! That went out with the sideshows. You know what sideshows at the circus are today, lady? Moon Walk, cotton candy, hot dogs, elephant rides. We got no fortune-tellers."

"We will take whatever work you have," Carlotta said quietly.

The man sighed and stepped down. "All right. You want to work the concession, lady? Cotton candy, caramel apples?"

"Yes."

"What about me?" asked Cory. "Can I feed the animals or something?"

"You'd like that, wouldn't you, kid? Son, I got no work for you. You just stay out of the way and I won't gripe." He turned back to Carlotta. "Be at the concession stand at four o'clock."

Macklin stepped back up into the trailer, but Carlotta stood fast. "Well, what is it?" he asked, with some annoyance.

"We will need a place to sleep," she said.

The man swore and tossed his toothpick away. "You got no trailer?"

Carlotta shook her head.

"All right, look. You sleep in the equipment trailer, the bright green one. I'm only doing this because you seem like a nice old gal and you been in the business. First sign of trouble, you're out. And if anything turns up missing from that trailer, I'll track your hides down from here to the coast. Got it?"

"We understand," said Carlotta.

10

It irked Cory that there was nothing for him to do with the circus. When they had the baking business, he was important. Carlotta wasn't up to running all over town to make deliveries and find new customers. She depended on him. And he could help with the baking, too.

But the concession stand was just a small trailer with a roll-up window for a counter. There wasn't room for an extra person in there. It was hard enough for Carlotta and Ike, the man who ran it, to stay out of each other's way.

The first show was at four-thirty. There had not even been enough time for them to go to the trailer Macklin said they could use. Carlotta wedged their bags beneath the sink and the ice machine and went to work. Cory hung around to watch. Ike was quick, and short on words. Cory wasn't sure Carlotta would be able to move fast enough to suit him. But there weren't too many customers in that first half hour.

Carlotta caught Cory's eye while twirling the soft blue cotton candy onto a paper cone. "Go on, go see the show," she whispered. "You make me nervous, watching like that."

He nodded and walked to the tent entrance, where the last customers were straggling in. The ticket collector looked at him expectantly.

"I don't have a ticket," Cory told him, "but my grandmother's working the concession stand."

"I don't know nothing about it," he said flatly. "You want in, you get a ticket or a pass from the boss."

Cory shoved his hands in his pockets and turned away. He wasn't about to ask any favors of Macklin and chance him throwing them out of the circus.

The midway that had been so full of life just moments ago was now deserted. From the tent came the buzzing of many voices, punctuated with explosions of laughter and applause. A band wove its melodies through the blended sounds. For a while, Cory lingered by the tent, listening and imagining what the various sounds might mean. But standing by the wall of canvas that separated him from the people and the fun made him feel lonely. Had he ever even been to a circus? He could not remember. He sighed and moved on.

He wandered back to the concession stand to

check on Carlotta. Ike was going over the trailer with a damp cloth, and Carlotta was restocking the tray of caramel apples. She looked ragged with fatigue. There was no place to sit down in there.

"You want me to take over for a while?" he offered.

Carlotta shook her head.

"Just while the circus is going on," said Cory.

Again Carlotta shook her head.

"You look beat," Cory continued. "Can't I get you something or help out in any kind of way?"

This time Carlotta gave a warning glance in Ike's direction, letting him know she didn't want Ike to hear.

"Well, see you around," said Cory. Lost and useless, he perched on the tongue of the trailer until the last of the applause burst in the air and the people came pouring out onto the midway. It was another busy time for the midway workers as they tried to squeeze the last dollars from the departing customers.

Then it was all over, and the midway was a ghost town strewn with drink cups, paper cones, caramel-apple sticks, and popcorn boxes.

Men in green jumpsuits—roustabouts, Cory guessed, remembering the word Carlotta had taught him—appeared and began spearing the trash with spiked poles and dropping it into plastic trash bags. Cory left his perch and began picking up trash.

Not long after, Eddie Macklin arrived, still

dressed in the high black boots, white pants, and red jacket of a ringmaster. He stopped, putting his hands on his hips, and watched Cory collecting trash.

"Hey, kid," he said after a moment.

"Sir?" Cory looked up.

"The next show is at seven thirty. At seven you go tell Ike I said set you up with a concession tray. But you remember, you're in there to hawk food, not to gape at the show."

"Yes, sir!" Cory exclaimed. "Thanks."

Macklin grunted in reply and walked toward the cluster of trailers on the edge of the grounds.

Bursting with news, Cory threw himself into collecting trash. Then he ran to the concession stand. Carlotta was just stepping down.

"Guess what, Grandma!" Cory cried, and he flushed with pride and pleasure.

Carlotta, despite her weariness, smiled. "What?"

"I was helping clean up the midway, and Mr. Macklin saw and gave me a job selling food during the next show!"

"That is wonderful. You have shown yourself a willing worker and changed his heart."

Cory hunched up his shoulders, embarrassed and pleased by the compliment. "Now we both have jobs," he added, wanting to keep talking about it.

Carlotta only nodded. Cory stole a closer look at her. She was walking carefully and a little bent over, as if her back hurt her. Strands of her thick hair had pulled free of the ribbon with which she had tied it back. She passed a hand across her forehead, pushing the hair away from her face.

"Where are you going?" he asked.

"To the trailer. I need to lie down awhile."

"Are you all right?"

"Yes," she answered, allowing him to take the carpetbag from her. "I am only very tired."

They located the green trailer, opened the door at the rear, and peered in. It was stuffy inside. Running partway down the left side of the trailer was a pole that held half a dozen or so costumes. On the other side were hooks and compartments intended for storage. At the end sat a heavy, low platform and a small orange bicycle.

"There're no bunks," Cory said.

"This is the equipment trailer. We will have to live like equipment."

Carlotta, grasping Cory's shoulder with her left hand, stepped up into the trailer. "There will not be so much room here when they pack up tonight."

"Tonight?" Cory swung up into the trailer.

"We pack up after the last show tonight. In the morning we move on. That is the way it is with the circus. Packing, unpacking, performing, on and on and on. You will see what a job really is."

Cory set the carpetbag on the floor. Carlotta eased herself down beside it and began rearranging the bag's contents to make a pillow.

"Where are we going?" Cory wanted to know.

"A little town to the south. Bentmoor." She lay down on the strip of threadbare carpet that ran down the center of the trailer, putting her head on the carpetbag.

Cory thought suddenly of her clean white room at Miss Sybil's, of the shining hallways and the low trim lines of the building on the thick carpet of grass. "Can I get you anything?" he asked. "Some dinner?"

"I am sick from the smell of those sweet things." She closed her eyes.

"How about some milk—and some plain bread?"

"Yes, if you can find some milk. And, Cory, make sure I get up in a half an hour."

When he returned fifteen minutes later with milk and cold hamburgers begged from the circus cook, Carlotta was asleep. He set the food beside her and tapped her shoulder. "Carlotta?"

Carlotta's reply was shrouded in sleep. "Peter-John? Is it you, Peter-John?"

Cory, startled, rocked back on his heels. "Carlotta—Grandma—it's me, Cory."

Carlotta blinked her eyes and looked around the trailer and then up at Cory. She appeared to him, in that moment, fragile and bewildered as a little child. He wanted to reach out and take her hand, touch her hair, comfort her somehow. Then the moment passed, and she was Carlotta again. "Oh, Cory, I thought— what is this?" she asked, seeing the food.

"I brought you some dinner."

"Thank you for this," she said, and raised the paper cup of milk to her lips, holding it in both hands.

When the trailers began to roll at dawn, Cory and Carlotta jerked awake. Cory's muscles were aching. After selling snacks during the last show, he had helped pull the tent down and pack everything up. A night sleeping on the hard, cramped trailer floor had not given him much rest.

Carlotta leaned against a wooden box, her eyelids drooping. Around them were the sounds of things rattling and shifting. Cory hoped everything was securely placed.

Relieved when the motion finally stopped, he threw open the trailer door and breathed in the still-moist morning air. Carlotta seemed glad to get out of the stuffy trailer, too, but she sat down on the step and surveyed the scene. "They will put up the cook's tent first. Then there will be breakfast. This is a busy time for the roustabouts."

Cory glanced at a group of men opening a thick square of canvas. Someone else was bringing the stakes. "I'll go help them," said Cory, forgetting his tiredness. "I'll come back and get you for breakfast, okay?"

She nodded.

When the tent was raised and the smell of food drifted out into the air, Cory returned for Carlotta. In silence they walked to the cook's tent and accepted their cups of hot coffee and plates of scrambled eggs, sausage, and fried bread. It was mostly the roustabouts who came for breakfast; the performers had climbed back into their bunks after the trip and would prepare their own food later in their trailers.

Carlotta seemed uninterested in their surroundings, but Cory felt exhilarated to be in the company of these circus men. It was like a brotherhood.

Eddie Macklin stopped by and clapped Cory on the shoulder. "Saw you packing up last night," he said approvingly.

Cory flexed his back to locate the muscles made sore from carrying and heaving tent sections. He wished sore muscles were like scars. He would wear them as badges to show that he had worked alongside the men.

To Carlotta, Macklin said, "See Ike at the concession by nine." He strode away.

Cory's eyes followed the man until he sat down at the head of the table with his breakfast. "You know, Car—Grandma, I can see why you didn't want to leave the circus to get married," Cory stated. "I think I'm going to stick with the circus, too."

Carlotta's eyes passed over him briefly and then returned to the plate of food before her. "You do not miss your nice home, your foster mama and papa?" she asked finally.

"No! Why should I? I'm nothing to them." He didn't like Carlotta's reminding him of that old, left-behind world. It seemed to rob him of something. He jabbed at his fried bread with the prongs of his fork.

100

"I wished for a mama and papa who did not argue, a mama and papa who loved," she said quietly. "Do yours?"

Cory ignored her question. "I'm going to see if I can help put up the big tent," he said, getting up.

"I will be in the trailer resting. Wake me in an hour."

Cory felt uneasy. He wished Carlotta hadn't mentioned Michele and Dan. Now he couldn't stop thinking of them. He leaned against the trailer where the big tent had been put and saw Michele, awkward and hesitant, waving good-bye as he rode away in Ms. Hanks's county car. He saw Dan, his arm cocked back, ready to send the football hurtling toward him. He saw Michele handing him the curved, green cabbage leaf for Mr. T.

Something knotted in Cory's stomach. He imagined the sausage and fried bread sitting intact on a jiggly bed of scrambled eggs in his stomach.

Men were working all over the field, siting off spaces, carrying canvas bags, raising poles, driving stakes, feeding animals. They walked around and past Cory without stopping to speak. Suddenly Cory felt that he was an outsider. The whole operation could roll on without him as it had done in the past. No one would even notice if he were not there at all. He had only imagined that he belonged. The realization bore down on him. He wondered if he'd ever feel at home and a part of things anywhere.

Dejected, he wandered through the jungle of trailers. Suddenly there was nothing lonelier than a trailer. Loneliest of all was the equipment trailer where Carlotta rested among the costumes and show props. She did not belong there.

He watched the huge, lumbering elephants as they were led out of their pungent, hay-strewn trailers, each to be chained by a hind leg to a stake. They swung their great trunks and stepped from side to side, peering out at their restricted world with small, defeated eyes.

Somehow those tiny eyes, embedded in the gray, incongruous heads, reminded Cory of his turtle, Mr. T.

He watched the toy poodles, jumping and yapping their outrage at captivity. The horses, solemn and mute in their trailers, awaited the fresh morning air and their oats.

The lion snarled as he passed, as if he were angry at Cory's freedom. Cory stopped and stared. The beast paced back and forth in his cage. The cage allowed him only two steps in each direction. These he took in an unchanging rhythm. His muscled legs twitched as if showing his readiness for the movement denied him.

Cory thought of Mr. T pressed up against the corner of his box, his unblinking gaze on the cardboard walls. Suddenly Cory's eyes filled with tears. He began to run. Behind him the roars, the growls, the trumpeting seemed deafening. He forced his legs to stretch and spring, imagined them pacing off great bites of land between himself and the circus. He imagined his leg muscles long and sinewy, propelling him through time and space. The town of Bentmoor lay ahead, and getting to it was Cory's only thought.

Safe on the narrow streets, he made himself slow down and walk. It was important that he not attract attention, that he not appear out of place. He imagined that passers-by could see his heart drumming, bulging out cartoon style, and he zipped his jacket.

Ahead of him the American flag flapped in front of the post office. In his pants pocket, Cory's fingers found some coins. Their cool hardness was comforting. He went into the post office, bought a postcard, and carried it to the high table where a pen dangled on the end of a chain.

"Dear Michele and Dan," he wrote. "Please let Mr. T go back to his home in the woods."

Cory hesitated, rolling the pen in his fingers. "I'm okay," he added. "Hope you are, too. Cory."

He addressed the card and dropped it into the slot marked Out Of Town. He walked out of the post office and breathed in the morning air. It was as cooling and refreshing as a drink of water. He felt renewed somehow, and he smiled. Unzipping his jacket, he walked back toward the ball field and the jumble of circus trailers parked there.

"Where's your grandmother, boy?" called Ike, as Cory passed by the concession.

"Sleeping, I guess."

Ike frowned. "Well, it's nine thirty. Tell her to get a move on!"

Nine-thirty! Cory began to run. He'd heard Macklin tell Carlotta to be at the stand at nine! Suddenly confused, Cory stopped running. He couldn't remember where the trailer was parked. Then he spotted it and started off again like, he thought, a rat in a maze.

He flung the trailer door open, and there lay Carlotta on the floor, a heavy packing blanket pulled up over her shoulders. For a moment, fear streaked through him. He thought Carlotta was dead.

Cory swung up into the trailer and knelt beside her. He shook her shoulder. The bones felt like a handful of twigs. "Get up. It's nine thirty!" he said urgently.

"Let me sleep, will you, Sybil?" she mumbled.

That she had confused him with someone else twice frightened Cory. He spoke more insistently. "Carlotta, get up. You were supposed to be at the concession stand half an hour ago!"

Carlotta swept off the blanket and struggled to her feet. "An hour!" She looked angry. "You were going to wake me." She turned without another word and climbed down from the trailer.

Cory slumped to the floor, leaning against the trailer wall. The fringed and ruffled costumes passed over his eyes and then became a curtain between him and the rest of the trailer. He thought of Michele, her stomach rounded with the baby she carried, bending down to pick up the postcard from the floor after the mail carrier had dropped it through the slot. Her face would be crinkled with worry. One by one the muscles of her face would relax as she read. He was not dead. He had not been kidnapped. Had she worried about those things?

She'd call Ms. Hanks to tell her he was okay, that he'd written to her. "Wasn't that *nice* of him to write," Ms. Hanks would say.

Michele and Dan would talk about it at dinner. "That boy who stayed here awhile wrote today," Michele would say. "Good," Dan would answer. Then, after dinner, they'd take Mr. T down to the woods. Or maybe they'd just put him out the door and he would get smooshed by a car as he tried to find his way home.

They were scheduled for two days of performances in Bentmoor. The shows on the second day were even more crowded than those of the first, and they nearly filled the seats to capacity. Cory hadn't expected that in the little town of Bentmoor. Probably people came from towns for miles around to see the circus. It was a big event. Probably when you washed your car in Bentmoor, half the town would come to watch.

Before the last show, the crowd that filled the midway seemed to keep expanding—like a balloon, filled and then stretched thin by forcing more air into it, Cory thought. He wouldn't have been surprised to see it burst. Children went flying away from their parents, and then their parents reeled them back like yo-yos. For a moment Cory wished for enough money in his pocket and enough time to ride the elephant, to bounce on the Moon Walk, to let the blue cotton candy melt to sugar on his tongue.

He saw Carlotta only briefly when he went to fill and refill his concession tray. She did not speak, and he wondered if she was still sore at him for not getting her up in time that morning. But she was busy, matching Ike step for step, her face gray and grave.

Hawking food inside the tent was not without its advantages. There were times when he could not sell, like when Reynaldo started across the tightrope on his silver bicycle. The crowd was breathless then, every eye trained upon the same point. Or when Paco the Clown imitated Reynaldo with the little orange bike that broke into pieces as he started across the low wire. It seemed irreverent at those times to walk through the stands shouting, "Caramel apples! Get your fresh roasted peanuts!"

During those peak moments, Cory turned and watched the performance. It was the timing that impressed him the most. The way Reynaldo was there, hanging from the trapeze at the exact moment that the beautiful Imelda let go of her trapeze and came flying through the air toward his strong and waiting hands. How could she trust that he would be there, that he would catch her? To put her life in his hands that way, she must know him like she knew herself. Cory wondered if he could ever trust someone that much.

Then someone would call out, "Hey, son, how much for a candy apple?" and he would jerk back to reality, looking guiltily for Eddie Macklin.

By the end of the show, Cory was sweaty with exertion. The arch in his right foot pained him and he limped to the cashier to turn in the money he'd collected.

As he waited for the money to be counted, his mind was awash with ideas. Maybe he could apprentice himself to the lion tamer. He imagined himself walking confidently around the cage, the great beasts snapping to attention as he barked out commands. Or maybe there was something he and Carlotta could do together. Telling fortunes was too tiring, she'd said. But maybe they could whip up a magic act. He could make her disappear and appear. She could rest while he made her body rise in thin air and while he sawed her in half. Kid Cory the Magician, they could call him. Or maybe The Incredible Cory. People would really go for a grandmother-grandson act.

"You're two bucks short," the cashier announced. "It'll have to come out of your pay."

Cory shrugged. He did not want to worry about money now. He and Carlotta were both working. They'd be all right. Maybe they'd even get their own trailer one day. They could have their names written on the side in great swirling letters.

He moved away from the cashier's trailer. The midway was still mobbed. He wondered how long it would take to move them all out, so Carlotta and the others could rest. First they'd have to pack up. He'd tell Carlotta to go on back to the trailer and sleep, he decided. He could pitch in and help with the packing like before. No need for her to work herself ragged, he'd tell her.

The crowd before him seemed to be knotted around the concession stand. He was surprised they were still buying food, after all he'd sold during the show. He stopped to try to figure out the best way to get through the mass of people.

Then, as if the crowd was all one body and heard his unspoken wish, it pulled back and squeezed to the side. A red light flashed in Cory's face. With a jolt, Cory saw the orange and white of an ambulance as it pulled away.

Cory bolted into the crowd, parting the people with his hands like they were high weeds in a field. Ike was standing behind the concession stand, watching the ambulance bounce across the rutted ball field and onto the road.

Ike saw Cory and jerked back suddenly as if he'd

been slapped. "It's your grandma!" shouted Ike. "Gone to the hospital."

For one terrible moment, Cory's stricken eyes locked with Ike's. Then he took off running in the direction the ambulance had taken.

"She shouldn'ta been workin' here!" Ike called after him. "I told Eddie. You shouldn'ta let her!"

12

"What happened to my grandma?" Cory was breathless from his run to the hospital. By the time he'd gotten there the ambulance sat empty in the circular emergency-room entrance, its double doors standing open.

The woman at the desk peered at him over the tops of a small pair of glasses. "Who's your grandma, sugar?"

"Carlotta—" Cory realized with horror that he had never learned her last name.

"You mean the woman they brought in from the circus?"

Cory nodded and gulped. His heart felt like a throbbing lump that was rising up into his throat.

"The doctors are with her now, sugar. You'll just have to wait. You want to call your folks?"

Cory shook his head and backed away. A doctor strode down the hall and went through the doors to the emergency room. Cory craned his neck, trying to see inside before the door swung shut.

He remembered how lifeless Carlotta had appeared when she was sleeping on the trailer floor earlier. Was that some sort of sign? What could have happened to her? Ike had said Cory shouldn't have let her work. Was it his fault then? Carlotta would do what she wanted—he knew that. But she *had* told him circus life was hard. *He* was the one who had really wanted to do it. If it weren't for him, she would never have left her quiet white room at Miss Sybil's Shady Rest.

The woman at the desk went into the emergency room. A few minutes later she emerged and sat down in the seat next to Cory. "She's doing okay, sugar," the woman said. "She's got her eyes open and is talking to the doctors."

"What's the matter with her? Can she go—home?"

"Oh, I don't know. I expect they'll want to hold her awhile. Why don't you go on home and we'll call you."

"Hey, can we get some help here?" A man had come in with a small, whimpering child in his arms.

"I've got to go," the woman said. "You go on and don't worry."

Cory knew he would not leave the hospital until he found out what was wrong with Carlotta. He would sleep on the chairs and eat his meals from the vending machines, if necessary. You just didn't go off somewhere when your grandmother was sick.

Moments later the outside door opened and Eddie Macklin stepped in. Still wearing his ringmaster clothing, he looked garish and out of place under the gleaming hospital lights, like a cartoon character plunked down in the middle of a soap opera. For a moment, Cory wasn't sure he was real.

Macklin spotted Cory. "I gathered up your stuff from the equipment trailer," he said. He sat down beside Cory, setting the backpack and the carpetbag on the floor at his feet. Cory noticed the film of dust that had settled on the ringmaster's high-topped boots. He smelled faintly of sweat and sawdust and wild animals.

"What's wrong with her?" Macklin asked.

Cory shrugged and shook his head. He didn't want to talk with Macklin. He felt as if he were made of glass, as if something inside would shatter if he spoke. He had to move carefully—and, above all, not feel anything very much.

"Ike said she just keeled over in the middle of making cotton candy," Macklin went on. "She's an old gal. I probably shouldn't have given her the job."

Yes, it's *your* fault, Cory thought. I'm just a kid, but you should have known the job was too much for her. Cory imagined himself battering Macklin's broad, hard chest with his fists, pounding and pounding until he was exhausted. It would feel good. But he did not move; he just sat there staring at the ringmaster's dusty boots.

"I just felt sorry for her—for both of you; seemed like you had some trouble on you. And she was circus people." There was an empty silence. Macklin reached into his pocket and drew out an envelope, which he handed to Cory. "Both of yours. Plus five dollars severance pay, but . . ."

Cory looked up at the man. He didn't understand what Macklin was talking about.

"I figure you're going to need it," Macklin went on. "Don't spend it all on candy bars now. It'll take this and more to get started again."

Cory looked inside the envelope at the crinkled bills it contained. What Macklin was trying to tell him came into focus. "You mean you're leaving us?"

"Well, yeah." Macklin looked uncomfortable. "We got a schedule. We got to leave. Got to be in South Carolina in the morning."

"What are we supposed to do?" cried Cory.

Macklin looked quickly around the room. "I'd keep it down, boy, if you don't want everybody to know your business." Then he dropped his voice to a whisper Cory could barely hear. "I figure you're alone in the world with just your grandma. You don't want the wrong people to know that or they'll put you in a home somewhere. Then what would Grandma do?"

Cory clamped his mouth shut. Macklin was right.

The big man rose awkwardly. "Well, good luck,

boy. You take good care of her, hear?" And then he was gone.

If the circus was like a family, he and Carlotta were certainly not members of it, Cory thought bitterly. Macklin was dumping them as easily as the Nortons had dumped him or the Keppermans would have. As easily as his mother had when she'd had enough of him. Maybe it was his idea of family that was wrong—a phony thing he'd gotten from TV families who worked through a new problem every week and had everyone smiling by the end of the half hour.

Cory looked up to see a doctor approaching him. He was a paunchy, middle-aged man with streaks of gray running through his hair. His hands dangled into the deep white pockets of his jacket. "You must be Cory."

Cory pushed himself upward from the arms of the chair. "Yes."

"Well, your grandmother is all right." The doctor sat down in the chair beside him. "We're going to keep her a couple of days just to make sure."

"What happened to her?"

"She just fainted. It's not uncommon. Maybe she's been under some stress lately? Maybe she hasn't been eating as well as she might?"

Cory wasn't sure whether the doctor expected him to answer his questions. "If she's all right, why can't she leave?"

"We'd just like to keep an eye on her, make sure

there aren't any complications. It will be good for her to rest and build herself up again."

"Can I see her?"

"Better make it tomorrow. She's had enough excitement for one day."

The doctor rose and then turned back to Cory as if a thought had just occurred to him. "Should I be calling your parents about her?"

"Haven't got any parents."

"You stay with your grandmother?"

Cory nodded.

"Well, what will you do now?" asked the doctor. "You don't want to stay alone." His look was kind, almost fatherly, and Cory found it necessary to turn away. He wondered if his own father had ever looked at him that way. He searched for a memory of his father's face but could only find black leather.

"Have you got any relatives—an aunt or uncle you could stay with?" the doctor asked.

"Yeah," Cory agreed quickly. "I can stay with my aunt and uncle. They won't mind. In fact, I'd better go on over now."

Before the doctor could say another word, Cory was outside, alone in the darkness, with Carlotta's carpetbag, his knapsack, and no place to go.

13

Cory felt sure that an eleven-year-old boy alone in a strange town at night with luggage in hand was not a common sight; he had to do something to make himself less conspicuous. He wondered what Carlotta would have suggested.

A police car rolled up in front of the emergency entrance, and Cory stepped into the shadows. Without Carlotta he certainly looked like a runaway now. He had to steer clear of the police.

Bentmoor was a small town. Were there drunks and thieves in the abandoned buildings here, like Carlotta said there would be in Lanton? Did he stand a chance among them? He remembered the menacing, watchful eyes of the men in the rooming house they looked at. Maybe Eddie Macklin would let him stay in the equipment trailer one more night, before the circus moved on—No! He wouldn't ask Macklin for anything! They didn't need him and he didn't need them.

The bus station, he thought suddenly. He had seen it the other day on his way to the post office. That was the logical place for someone with luggage. Glancing about cautiously, he moved out of the shadows and headed toward it.

The place was nearly empty. He saw two men board a bus, and when another bus came in, one man got off and quickly left the station.

Cory left his backpack on. Pushed up high as he settled on the long wooden bench, it became his pillow. He linked his arms through the handles of Carlotta's carpetbag, hugging it so that no one could take it from him as he slept.

He was just feeling his eyelids droop with sleepiness when the man at the ticket counter called him.

"Sir?"

"You waitin' on a bus?" The small mustachioed man peered anxiously at him over his bifocals.

"Yes, sir," he replied.

"Well, which one? The one to Akron or to New York?"

"Akron."

"You want to buy your ticket? I'm fixing to close up. Won't be anyone in till six-thirty A.M."

"Uh . . ." Cory hadn't counted on this. "Uh, my uncle—he's gone to get the money. I left it at home."

The man sighed. "Well, you can buy a ticket from

the driver, then. I'm not going to stay open till your uncle gets back. Don't know what anybody's thinking of, leaving a boy here late at night," he muttered, "but it's not my responsibility."

The man pulled the iron grate down over the counter and locked it. Cory drew his feet up onto the bench and settled back. In a few minutes the man left, and Cory was alone. He looked uneasily about the dimly lit waiting area and then moved to a bench against the wall where he wouldn't be as easily seen from the window.

When he awoke at 6:00 A.M., he felt he had not slept at all. Afraid someone might find him there alone and take what little he had, he'd awakened periodically all through the night. His eyes were sleep-bruised.

He stood up, adjusting the pack on his back, and left the station before anyone could question him. At least Carlotta was sleeping in a bed. That was good.

The doctor had said he could see her today. He headed for the hospital. Visiting hours, the woman at the desk told him firmly, began at 10:00 A.M.

Cory sat down in the lobby. It would be a long wait, and he was beginning to get hungry. He walked into the rest room and surveyed his face. His eyes looked pink and puffy, and there were smudges on his cheeks. He washed his face and hands.

There would be a cafeteria in the hospital, but that would be more expensive than a grocery. Carlotta had taught him that. He smiled at himself. He was doing okay, he decided. He'd spent a night alone, and he knew where to find a cheap meal. Carlotta would be proud of him.

By ten Cory was back at the hospital. The woman at the desk gave him a visitor's card and told him how to find Carlotta's room. He walked slowly down the hall, watching his reflection in the shining floor. He was almost afraid to look up, to glimpse into the rooms of the ill.

Carlotta had called the nursing home the house of death. Was that what the hospital was, too? He wondered if Carlotta was really all right. Maybe the doctor hadn't leveled with him because he was a kid.

Finally, Cory had to look up to turn to the hall on the left and walk two doors down to Carlotta's room. He sucked in his breath and went in.

The curtains were drawn around the first bed and, for a moment, Cory didn't know what to do. You couldn't knock on a curtain. Then, softly, he said, "Grandma?"

"Cory? I'm in the second bed."

Cory breathed out his relief and passed the drawn curtains. Carlotta raised herself up against the big white pillow. Cory was taken aback at how small and delicate she seemed lying there, her thick gray-and-white hair splayed out on the pillow.

"How're you feeling?" he asked. He felt awkward with her suddenly, as if her being in the hospital had somehow changed her. He felt that he should have brought her something—flowers or candy. Instead, he held out the carpetbag. "I brought you this."

She smiled wanly. "Just put it by the bed. I have not been much help to you."

"That's not true. Last night I figured out I should stay at the bus station by asking myself what you would do. And this morning I got breakfast for seventy-five cents." He slipped his backpack off his shoulders and drew out a partially crushed box. "Pop-tarts," he said. "There's still one left. You want it?"

She shook her head. "The circus?"

"Went to South Carolina."

"Ah. Of course."

There was a silence, which Cory rushed to fill. "Who's next door?" he asked, jerking his thumb toward the drawn curtains.

"Mavis Jones. They were giving her a bath and her heart stopped."

"Oh." Cory gulped. "The doctor told me you were getting out right away."

"Yes. But it will always be something, Cory. I am at that age," she said dully. "Maybe I should go back to Sybil's where I will not be a bother to anyone."

Cory shrugged this off. "You're not a bother to anyone," he said. "We'll figure something out. It doesn't have to be the circus. We could start our bakery again."

Carlotta shook her head. "And poison our customers with salt bread?"

Again, Cory ignored her objections. "I thought of
a new kind of Pop-tart. It has bubble gum inside.
After you eat breakfast, the gum—it's sugar free—
the gum cleans your teeth!"

A smile twitched at her lips. Encouraged, Cory
took her hand and turned it palm up. "I see Grasshopper Bakery with franchises all over the East Coast.
Even the White House orders poppy-seed bread for
the president and the first lady. For their children,
they order bubble gum Pop-tarts."

"I am the fortune-teller." She slipped her hand
out of Cory's and turned his hand palm-up. "I see a
bright boy with no home. A boy who should be in
school. I see a man and woman who want him to be
their child."

Angrily, Cory jerked his hand away. "You don't
see that! What are you trying to pull?" After all
they'd been through together, was she backing out on
him? Why? Maybe she was tired of him, he thought
darkly. Maybe they didn't belong to each other after
all. Or maybe she was just scared.

A nurse leaned into the room. "Problem?"

Cory looked at Carlotta. Her eyes were fixed on
him. He looked at the nurse. "No problem," he mumbled. "I was just leaving." He turned and brushed
past her.

Halfway down the hall, he stopped. Even in his

anger, he couldn't leave her like that, helpless in bed. He went back to her room. "I'm going to figure out something for us. You'll see."

He left as the orderly wheeled in an empty bed and put it where Mavis Jones should have been.

14

"Ms. Hanks?" Cory scratched the back of one leg with his other foot. Calling his social worker was the last resort. But it was all he could think of to do for Carlotta.

"Cory?"

"You said I could call you collect if I ever needed to." In his right hand Cory held the small card that had been tucked away in the pocket of his backpack. It read: Patsy Hanks, M. S. W., Foster Care, Pemberton County Social Services, and there was an address and phone number.

"Yes, of course, Cory. Where are you?"

"Never mind where I am." He shifted his weight, leaning his shoulder against the glass walls of the telephone booth. Her voice sounded bright, but tense, as if she were in a hurry about something. Cory had the feeling she might come bursting out of the receiver at any moment and grab him. It made him want to run.

"I'm okay," he told her. "But I'm worried about Carlotta."

"Carlotta?" Ms. Hanks sounded puzzled. "That old lady from the nursing home? Is she with you, Cory?"

Cory chewed his lower lip. He wondered if it had been a mistake to call her. "She's in a hospital. But she's okay. She's going to get out soon and she needs a place to stay."

"Well, Miss Sybil's—"

"She's not going back there." Cory cut her off. "That place is no good. If she has to go there, then we're not coming back."

"Okay, okay," Ms. Hanks said urgently. "She doesn't have to go there. I have a friend in gerontology. I'm sure she can work something out."

"Okay, you talk to her. It has to be a place where she can do what she wants. Where she can bake, and see friends, and people won't be butting into her business." He wondered if there was such a place. Hadn't his foster homes sounded great until he'd moved in? Ms. Hanks could make even the children's shelter sound like summer camp.

"I'll call you later," Cory told her. "You can tell me what your friend says then." Cory had it all worked out. He'd seen this sort of thing on TV lots of times. He was like a kidnapper calling a family. Only he wasn't after money—just a good home for his grandmother.

"Cory, wait! Don't hang up! The Keppermans, they're worried sick—"

"They are?"

"Yes. They went off to look for you. They said they had an idea where you were, but they wouldn't tell me where."

"I have to go," Cory said, and hung up the phone. He let out a big breath and stared at the receiver. He wondered if Ms. Hanks had talked so much because she was having the phone bugged. He imagined a burly police officer standing by her desk, doing something to the phone while Ms. Hanks desperately tried to keep him talking. But no—she wouldn't have been able to get a cop the first time he called.

So the Keppermans were looking for him. He gazed out on the streets of Bentmoor, half expecting to see them walking toward him. Michele's face would be sad and serious. Dan would be excited, maybe angry.

But why should they be looking for him? Maybe they were in trouble because he'd run away. The county would be pretty mad about that. That could explain Ms. Hanks's tension on the phone—she was probably in trouble, too. He wondered if his picture was on a poster of missing kids. Maybe there was a reward offered for him. Maybe there had been search parties. He rather liked the idea of all those people worried and searching for him. But he'd been slick;

he'd stayed one step ahead of them, frustrating their efforts at every turn. But what made Michele and Dan think they knew where he was?

Cory opened the glass door and stepped out of the telephone booth. He would wait until afternoon to call Ms. Hanks, to make sure she had time enough to talk with her friend about Carlotta. What he had to do now was find a place to spend the night. He couldn't go back to the bus station; the ticket man thought he was in Akron, wherever that was.

He began to walk through the town, looking up alleyways and behind stores. Other kids were in school, he realized. He'd have to be careful; it wouldn't do to let a cop see him and ask a lot of questions.

Ahead of him Cory saw a river crossed by a bridge. Carlotta had talked about sleeping under bridges, he remembered. He glanced about him and trotted toward it. Crouching, he walked underneath.

Under the bridge was a wedge of ground where hill met concrete and sloped down to the river. To this spot someone had dragged a large piece of cardboard. Cory sat down on it and thought. There was some protection from the wind, but not much. It would be cold. He could handle it for a night or two, he decided, but Carlotta couldn't. If Ms. Hanks really found a good home for her, he'd take her there. Then he'd leave again. Like Robin Hood, he would slip back from time to time to visit her. It would be risky. Soon enough they would know he was seeing her and lay a trap for him. The county didn't like its kids getting away. And if Carlotta didn't like the new place . . .

Maybe they could both go to California, instead. Someplace warm. They could start the bakery again.

A gust of wind tossed the treetops along the riverbank and whooshed beneath the bridge. Cory got up, wrapping his arms around himself for warmth. Where did that cardboard come from, he wondered. Did that mean somebody was already sleeping under the bridge? Cory shivered, but not from the cold this time. He'd have to approach the bridge carefully that night and see who might have already claimed the spot.

The day passed slowly for Cory. After lunch, he went back to the hospital to see Carlotta. She had saved him a dish of pudding and a roll from her lunch.

"No, thanks," said Cory. He felt funny about taking food from her when she was the one in the hospital. "I got a package of day-old bologna from the grocery for lunch."

"Eat it," Carlotta insisted. "The pudding has milk, and you need grain, too."

Reluctantly, Cory bit into the roll.

"Where are you sleeping tonight?"

"Oh, I got a place," he said vaguely. He remembered that, although he'd gotten the bridge idea from Carlotta, she hadn't seemed to think it was a good place to stay.

She pursed her lips. "This is no kind of life for a boy."

"Sure it is. It's like—like Huck Finn." With a mouth full of roll, he managed a grin to show her how good he thought his life was.

"The doctor says I may leave tomorrow."

This time Cory's grin was genuine. "Really?" He swallowed the mouthful of roll. "How about leaving today?" If she got out today, they could head right for California. He wouldn't have to meet up with whoever owned the cardboard.

"He wants to watch my heart a little longer," she said. "Because of that attack I had. I have to take it slow and easy, Cory. And eat better, too."

She'd never make it to California, Cory realized. It was too hard a trip. And there would be a lot of winter days to get through between Bentmoor and California. She was frail. Her body made barely more than a wrinkle under the blanket. He set the pudding back on the table. "I'm full," he lied. "You're gonna have to eat this."

He'd have to find them a place here in Bentmoor, he decided. Maybe they could get a room for the money they'd earned at the circus. But they'd have to make more money right away. There was the bakery. And in the winter he could shovel snow. Come spring there'd be cars to wash.

The more he thought about calling Ms. Hanks back, the more he thought it was a bad idea. Ms. Hanks had him popping in and out of homes where he wasn't wanted. What made him think her friend would do any better for Carlotta? And they'd be separated.

Carlotta interrupted his thoughts. "Did you think about what I said this morning?"

For a moment, Cory couldn't figure out what she was talking about. Then he remembered their argument. She had been trying to persuade him to give up, go back to the Keppermans. But they didn't want him. Why couldn't he make her understand that? "I don't want to think about it," he said tightly.

"I was selfish to go away with you. I thought only how I hated Miss Sybil's, not of all the things you would be giving up."

"I didn't give up anything I cared about!" Cory retorted. "Anyway, I came and got you, remember?" He knew he shouldn't argue with someone who had heart trouble, but he couldn't help himself.

"Maybe if you had had more time with those people—those foster parents—you would have cared about them."

"No I wouldn't. They didn't care about me. They were getting ready to kick me out!" If she was going to keep after him, he thought bitterly, he'd have to stop visiting her.

"I left school at sixteen, Cory," she said. "It was not a good thing. And you are only eleven."

"I said I don't want to talk about it!" Cory snatched up his backpack and hurried out of the room. Fuming, he strode, head down, through the hall toward the lobby. It wasn't until he heard his name called that he stopped and looked up.

There in the lobby stood Dan and Michele. For

one frozen moment he stared at them as if unable to believe his eyes. Then he bolted for the door, running out across the parking lot and onto the lawn.

He heard Dan running behind him, calling as he came. Then Dan's arms were around his waist, tackling him. The evening at the school yard flashed before him, he and Dan rolling down the hillside together, the sense of belonging. But this time Dan didn't knock him to the ground. He held Cory, kicking and flailing, in his arms.

"Whoa, boy!" cried Dan, panting. "I'm not gonna hurt you. We just want to talk."

"You can't make me go back to the children's shelter!"

"Nobody's gonna make you go anywhere, Cory. Just let us talk, and then if you don't want to go home with us we'll leave you here."

"Really?"

"Yes, really. Can I let you go now? You won't run on me?"

"Okay."

Dan released him, and Cory took a step backward, out of Dan's reach. By that time Michele had caught up to them. Cory was surprised that, although over a month had passed since he'd seen her, she still looked trim. He wondered when she would start looking round like other pregnant women he'd seen.

"Cory." She touched his arm hesitantly. "We've been so worried. What made you run away like that? Did I do something to upset you?"

"I just saved you the trouble of sending me back to the shelter, is all. You don't need me, so I don't need you, either." Furious, he felt tears sting at his eyes.

"Sending you back—why would we send you back?" Dan sounded surprised.

"You're gonna have a baby. I heard you," Cory returned. "You're going to have a *real* family, so what do you want with me?"

"We kind of hoped you'd be a big brother to the baby," Dan told him. For a moment, Dan's face reminded him of the doctor's—kind and fatherly.

Cory was stunned. Was it really true that they hadn't planned to send him away? In his heart, Cory felt a shaking and a crumbling. "What about school? You were pretty mad about that."

"Hey, we didn't expect you not to have problems. Everybody has problems. Sure, we got upset about what was going on with you, but that's what parents do. That doesn't mean we wanted to send you back."

A voice within Cory cried out, That's what parents do? I thought parents gave up on you when you were a problem. I thought— He wanted to cry like a baby. He wanted to curl up right there on the grass and weep. Would they hold him if he did?

"Oh, Cory." Michele swallowed hard. "We hoped to adopt you. Ms. Hanks said we should have you as a foster child first, to see if it would work for all of us. Maybe you wouldn't have been happy, but we never would have sent you back, unless you wanted to go."

Michele wound her sweater around herself, crossing her arm over her chest. She glanced at Dan and went on. "I guess I didn't do a very good job of making you happy. I—I grew up in a girls' home, Cory. No one ever came to take me out of there. I promised myself I'd get at least one kid out of one of those places—more, if I could. That's why Dan and I bought that big old crazy-looking house. To fix up, to fill up. I never had a mother. I guess I don't make much of a mother myself."

The vision of Michele standing on the doorstep waving good-bye to him flashed in his mind again. He remembered her sitting on the couch, looking sad and uncertain, when she and Dan talked to him about his schoolwork. "You didn't do so bad," he said huskily. "How'd you find me, anyway?"

"Your postcard," said Dan. "The postmark said Bentmoor. We had about given up on finding you, though. We called Ms. Hanks to let her know, and she told us to check the hospital."

"I'd been feeding your turtle, Cory," Michele said. "I was going to keep him for when you came back."

When he came back. They really had been waiting for him to return, then. Saving his place, feeding his pet. Waiting. Expecting him. "Did you take him back to the woods?"

Michele hesitated. "He died. He just wouldn't eat."

Carlotta was right, Cory thought. All Mr. T ever

wanted was to be free. That's all anybody wanted, Carlotta said. Were he and Carlotta free? Free to scrounge around each day for food and a place to sleep. Maybe that was freedom for a turtle, but it wasn't freedom for him. He didn't feel free dodging police, afraid to stay in one place too long, worrying about how to get money. He let his backpack slide off his shoulders and held it in his two hands.

"Ms. Hanks told us about your friend Carlotta. Is she going to be all right?"

"She's—my grandmother. We sort of adopted each other." He felt his face redden. "She's okay. She'll be getting out tomorrow."

"However did you two get by?" Michele wanted to know.

Michele's questions seemed to cast warmth upon him. He wanted to bask in it. "We worked with the circus awhile. And before that we had a bakery business in Lanton. Carlotta knows how to make all kinds of great things from different countries." As he told it, he had the sensation of telling about an exciting movie he'd seen. It all seemed slightly removed from himself, and long ago.

"We'd like to take you home with us," Dan said.

"You know, from making Carlotta your grandmother, that you don't have to be blood relatives to care." Michele's eyes, when she glanced quickly at him, tugged at something deep and strong within him. "We want to be family to you, Cory," she said.

Cory thought of the big old wooden house that

was their home. He imagined himself stretched out on that comfortable bed in the room that he'd called his, listening to Dan and Michele as they moved about the living room. He pictured Michele's needlepoint HOME SWEET HOME in the entryway. He thought of the straight, orderly streets and the square green lawns, twilight descending about them like a mist, and the lights clicking on like bright yellow balls in the houses.

"I can't leave Carlotta," he said, looking at his feet. "I've got to find her a home. Miss Sybil's stinks, and she doesn't need a nursing home, anyway. She just needs a friend around and a kitchen to use." Being family wasn't easy, he was thinking. Sometimes it meant standing by someone even though they'd made you angry. Sometimes it meant stepping away when a carpet was suddenly rolled out like a golden pathway before you, when arms were beckoning.

Michele was silent a moment, and then she looked at her husband. "Dan?"

Dan seemed to read her thoughts. He shrugged in assent. "We've got the room."

Michele turned to Cory. "Maybe Carlotta could stay with us."

"She could stay there until she found something better," said Dan.

"Or maybe—maybe it'd just work out for all of us." Michele turned to Dan. "It sounds like she doesn't have anybody, either, Dan. Maybe she wouldn't like it, with the baby and the noise, though. Maybe she wouldn't like *us*."

Cory caught his breath. "You mean we could both live there?"

"We could sure try it," said Dan. "It's what we always said we'd do—make a real home for people who needed it. We'd always thought of kids, but I don't see why it couldn't be an older person."

Would Carlotta want to do it, Cory wondered, or would she call it begging? "She'd probably want to pay for her room," Cory said. "She likes to carry her own weight."

Michele nodded. "Or maybe she could help me with the cooking and baking. I never had anyone to teach me. Maybe she could be a foster grandma to the baby, since I can't give it grandparents."

"And I know a foster mother who could use a foster mother of her own, honey," Dan said pointedly to Michele. He squeezed her shoulder gently. "Besides, what's not to like?"

Michele stuffed her hands into her pockets, drawing her shoulders up around her ears. Just like Mr. T, ducking into his shell, thought Cory. She's scared! The thought hit Cory with the force of a revelation. She *wants* Carlotta to be like a mother, but she's afraid it won't work. Cory wished suddenly to throw his arms around her. Wishing it so powerfully made him ache. He shoved his hands into his jacket pockets and then self-consciously drew them out again, letting them dangle at his sides. Dan put his arm around

Cory's shoulders. With his free hand he took Cory's backpack and slung it over his own shoulder. "Let's go ask Carlotta."

They were okay, Michele and Dan, Cory thought as they walked back toward the hospital. They seemed to really mean what they said. Maybe it was safe to let the good feelings he had about them come.

It was funny how easy it was for Dan to show he liked you, and how hard for Michele. He and Michele were sort of alike, he decided—nervous about feeling their feelings. Afraid they'd get hurt. And like Carlotta, who got mad at you sometimes because she wanted so much to make everything right for you. Because she loved you so much and didn't know how to just say so.

Experimentally, Cory laid a hand lightly on Michele's shoulder. Her arm, when she curved it around his back, was warm and comforting.